Books by Joy Nash

The Nephilim Series
The Night Everything Fell Apart

Demons and Angels (2017)

Druids of Avalon Series
Celtic Fire

The Grail King

Deep Magic

Silver Silence

Immortals Series
The Awakening

The Crossing

Blood Debt

also by Joy Nash
A Little Light Magic

Christmas Unplugged

Looking for a Hero

www.joynash.com
extras, excerpts
behind the book secrets

Praise for Joy Nash

Silver Silence

"Spellbinding! Joy Nash combines her knowledge of Celtic lore with timeless legends and writes breathtaking romance of unconditional love amid a backdrop of lush descriptions and powerful magic." ~*Paranormal Romance Reviews*

The Grail King

A Romantic Times TOP PICK! "Not since Mary Stewart's *Merlin Trilogy* has the magic of Avalon flowed as lyrically off the pages." ~*RT BOOK Reviews Magazine*

A Little Light Magic

"One of those books that when you finish reading it, you have to turn around and start it all over again." ~*Bitten by Books*

The Crossing

"Splendidly entertaining." ~*Booklist* on *The Crossing*
"Mac's personality is in full blaze. It is impossible not to fall in love with this man!" ~*Romance Junkies*

Looking for a Hero

"Oh man! A hilarious ride that had me falling out of my seat with laughter... Don't miss this story." ~*Romance Reviews Today*

Looking for a Hero

Joy Nash

JOYNASH BOOKS
Doylestown PA

Looking for a Hero
Copyright © 2013 by Joy Nash
ISBN 978-1-941017-03-6
Published by: joynash books, llc
Doylestown PA, USA
Cover design by StoryWonk
Interior design by Joy Nash
Christmas Unplugged
Excerpt Copyright © 2013 by Joy Nash

First Paperback Edition: October 2016

To Jim,
my hero,

Wednesday, 10:47 pm
Three days, one hour, thirteen minutes, and counting...

Oh, man. It was his lucky day. An original 1951 Action Comics #158, The Kid from Krypton, shimmered enticingly, nineteen minutes from closing on eBay.

Yes! Clark Kendall raised both arms in a two-fisted salute to the superhero gods. He'd lusted after this particular Superman comic book for ages. Now it was as good as his.

He typed in his bid the old-fashioned way: on his laptop keyboard. It launched into cyberspace just as he became aware of the sound of a chirping bird, followed by the drone of an airplane, coming from the cordless phone at his elbow. He made a point of reprogramming the office ringtone whenever he was on desk duty.

He hit the answer button. "Heroes United For Freedom... Yeah, we deliver... Go ahead..."

He shifted the phone to one shoulder as he watched the eBay screen refresh. "One roast beef hero sandwich, no onions... one Italian hero, hold the mayo... Drinks with that?... Two Cokes... Your address?... Right. Got it. Twenty minutes."

He cut the connection, wondering how long it would be before the hungry customers figured out their dinner wasn't coming. It was amazing, really. Somehow, even with absolutely no advertising and an unlisted phone number, the fake New York-style sub shop four levels above his head still managed to attract business. It almost made him want to open a take-out joint in Newark, New Jersey for real.

Almost, but not quite.

He pushed his glasses up the bridge of his nose and squinted at the laptop screen. Damn. Someone had topped his bid. He typed in a counter offer and sent it scurrying across the broadband connection.

"Hey, Clark."

He swiveled his chair toward the door, swallowing hard. Diana Price had come looking for him? More luck. That only happened in his dreams.

He held his breath as the shapely Amazonian princess sashay the HUFF control room, forty-four-and-a-half double D's all but exploding from her star spangled corset. When she leaned over the back of his chair and brushed her breasts against his shoulders, he nearly turned blue and passed out.

"What'cha doing?" she asked, leaning over his shoulder. Her breath tickled his ear.

Trying desperately to breathe, Clark thought, but masculine pride prevented him from announcing that little bit of information.

"I'm on eBay," he told her. "I put in a bid on a Superman comic book."

"Think you'll get it?"

He twisted his neck, angling for a better view of her

boobs without being too obvious. Did he think he'd get it? From Diana? No, but a man could dream.

"Clark? You okay?"

He gave himself a mental shake. "Yeah, fine. Listen," he said, forcing a casual tone. "My shift's almost done. You want to go out for a drink afterward?"

Diana's red lips quirked knowingly at him. Too knowingly. He knew he was toast even before she started laughing.

"I can't." She presented him a smile reserved for children, puppies, and guys who were about to get the shaft. "I've got a date with Bruce."

Clark's fist closed on the computer mouse so tightly it was a wonder the thing didn't let out a squeal. Bruce Wynn, superhero. Scratch that. Superjerk.

"He's just using you for sex," Clark said.

Diana only laughed. "I know! That's what makes it fun." She gave him a little hug. "Aw, Clark, are you jealous? That's so sweet."

He felt his cheeks heat. Sweet. Yeah, just what every superhero aspired to.

As if on cue, Bruce appeared at the door, arms crossed over his steroid-enhanced chest. Muscles bulged under his gray spandex shirt and black tights. He wasn't wearing his cape at the moment, but Clark could almost see the shiny black fabric flapping in an imaginary breeze.

Bruce gave an infinitesimal nod in Diana's general direction. "Babe." His moody gaze shifted the tiniest bit to the right. "Clark."

Diana rushed across the room, gushing a reply. Clark's stomach turned slightly nauseous. Sure, Bruce was something to look at—and if you believed half the rumors, a veritable god in bed—but was that all a woman wanted in a guy? You'd think rock hard abs, a perfect profile, and a bottomless supply of gloomy angst would get old after a while.

Bruce and Diana melded into a liplock. Clark pushed his glasses up the bridge of his nose and turned back to eBay. Only two minutes left, and he'd been knocked off the top again. Hell. He upped his bid into four figures and sent it flying. No way was he going to let this one go.

The phone rang again.

"Heroes United For Freedom," Clark droned, then snapped to attention when Captain Marvelous' radio announcer baritone boomed across the line.

"Clark, round up the troops. We've got a situation."

"A situation, Captain?"

From the corner of his eye, he saw Bruce and Diana disengage.

"Can't say any more on an unsecured line, son, but I can tell you the outlook is not good. Not good at all."

Was it ever?

"Tell every hero we've got on the books to report to my ready room in one hour."

Whoa. Clark couldn't remember the last time The Captain had ordered a full HUFF assembly. This was major. A dire threat to life as they all knew it, most likely.

His gaze drifted back to eBay. Damn. His mysterious

opponent had topped his bid two seconds before the countdown expired. The Kid from Krypton was history.

It looked like Clark's luck had run out.

Wednesday, 11:00 pm
Three days, one hour, and counting...

Yes!

Blossom Breeze sprang to her feet and did a little victory dance around her chair. That last minute bidder had come out of nowhere. She'd practically broken out in a cold sweat, but somehow she managed to squeak in under the wire to win the eBay bid for Action Comics #158, *The Kid from Krypton*. She'd only been looking for that particular issue *forever*. After it was framed, she'd hang it on her wall right between her signed portraits of Christopher Reeve and Dean Cain.

She collapsed in her chair and beamed at the screen. Life was perfect.

A nanosecond later, a chat message popped up on her screen.

<Hey, Blossom>

Bernie. Okay, well maybe life wasn't completely perfect.

<Hey, Bernie> she typed back, mentally adding the emoticon for rolling eyes. Bernie was sitting on the other side of the cubicle partition on her left, less than five feet away.

Another geek occupied the cubicle to her right. Oh, sure, she could put a positive spin on things and say she spent every night surrounded by single men under thirty, but where would that get her? She'd still be right here in the computer lab at Megalopolis Polytechnic Institute.

She sighed as a series of numbers materialized in her chat window. Another one of Bernie's freaking mathematical cryptograms. A second later, his head popped up over the partition, all bright eyes and big ears.

"Well, what do you say?"

Blossom squinted at Bernie's coded message, but it was late, and it'd been a tough day. The encryption could've spelled out "Do you want to get naked?" and she wouldn't even have known.

Hey. Wait a minute...

She blinked at the screen, mentally decoding: *Do you want to...*

A sudden vision of a naked Bernie seared her brain, doing instant damage to all major synapses. Oh, please. No. Anything but that. Bernie weighed all of one hundred and thirty pounds, soaking wet. Naked or clothed, no thank you.

Tentatively, she deciphered the rest of the code. *...go to the Star Trek convention tomorrow?*

Her breath left in a rush. Thank you, God.

"So? Do you?" Bernie's goofy grin stretched from ear to ear, his tongue lolling out of his mouth, puppy dog style. No doubt he thought encrypted chat message propositioning a very clever way to procure female companionship.

"Brent Spiner's going to be there," he said in a

wheedling tone.

Blossom gave him a thin smile. "I'd love to, Bernie. I really would. But tomorrow's not good for me." She had to feed her goldfish. And wash her hair. And visit her gynecologist. "Maybe some other time."

"Geez, that's too bad. A bunch of us are going to my place afterwards for a TNG marathon."

TNG, Blossom knew only too well, was Geekspeak for *Star Trek, The Next Generation.* As in Picard, Data, Geordie and the gang.

"Sorry. I'll have to pass."

"Your loss," Bernie said, and ducked back into his cell.

Sighing, Blossom logged off and shut down. Bernie wasn't a bad guy, really. You could even make the case that his brain made up for what he lacked in physique. Of course, that was pretty much true of all the guys lurking in the bowels of the MPI computer department.

Call her shallow, but Blossom just couldn't seem to get past appearances when it came to men. She preferred guys with muscles. Lots of muscles, bulging out all over. She drooled over sculpted pecs and corded biceps. She spun elaborate fantasies starring hunk who looked like the superheroes on her apartment walls.

Which could only be termed an ironic twist of fate, since Blossom's off-the-charts IQ and meticulous coding talents had dumped her squarely into geekdom. In her world, men who fit the superhero mold were very few and extremely far between.

Wasn't life a bitch?

Thursday, 12:13 am

Two days, twenty-three hours, forty-seven minutes, and counting...

Clark couldn't remember the last time he'd seen Captain Marvelous looking so grim.

In his long and illustrious career as CEO of HUFF, The Captain had faced down more no-win situations than a marriage counselor. He excelled at snatching victory from the jaws of defeat, and then landing a square punch to the aforementioned jaws, shattering all its teeth. His keen mind and unerring instinct invariably chose just the right superhero talent needed to neutralize each dire threat that came across the hotline.

Clark shifted in his seat, trying to catch the faint breeze wafting from the overhead vent. When you crammed twenty-seven muscle-bound superheroes—and a few super-busty superheroines—into a small conference room, you tended to overload the air conditioning system. Too bad the HUFF ready room was three levels underground. Clark would've emptied his bank account for an open window. A little air freshener wouldn't come amiss, either.

Bruce Wynn sat right up front, of course, shooting the room's testosterone level right off the scale. As far as Clark was concerned, the guy didn't even belong in HUFF. Bruce didn't have any real superpowers. He was all cash, flash, and gadgets. Without his daddy's fortune and his cutting-edge technology, Bruce would be just another pretty face in the unemployment line.

Clark unzipped his laptop case and eased open his computer. He was HUFF's official secretary, partly because he was the only hero in the organization capable of stringing words into coherent sentences, and partly because his specialized psychic superpowers made it easy for him to take notes. He sent a burst of mental energy into the computer, causing the hard disk to whir in response. Bruce glanced over, frowning, as if the sound irritated him.

Suck it, buddy.

Captain Marvelous took his position at the podium. Clark sat up straighter in his seat and gave HUFF's fearless leader his full attention.

"Thank you all for arriving at such short notice," The Captain said. "I won't beat around the bush, because frankly, we haven't much time. Our operatives in the field have just uncovered a DP of massive proportions."

Clark and the entire assembly of superheroes gave up a collective gasp. DP was superhero slang for "Diabolical Plot." DP's were perpetrated by EMG's, or "Evil Maniacal Geniuses." Clark shook his head. You just never knew when an EMG would snap. When one did, it wasn't pretty.

Captain Marvelous cleared his throat. "According to my sources, Lex Loser's tenuous hold on sanity has finally crumbled. He's retreated to a secret underground lair and is preparing to detonate a computerized neutron bomb. He intends to kill the entire population of Earth—without damaging its resources. After the explosion, he'll live in luxury, attended by the army of robotic servants he's stolen from the Japanese government." The Captain exhaled heavily. "We've been caught flat-footed on this one, folks. The bomb is set to go off Saturday at midnight."

A horrified buzz zapped back and forth across the room. Lex Loser was an EMG known to be capable of perpetrating the worst atrocities, but this DP far surpassed any evil he'd previously conceived. Clark concentrated on thought-streaming his notes onto the computer even as his blood turned to ice in his veins.

Back in the last row, young Peter Parkington jumped up so quickly he almost dropped his camera. "I volunteer to take Lex down, Captain!"

Captain Marvelous shook his head, his thick shock of white hair catching the overhead fluorescents in a lens-flare effect. "I'm sorry, kid. Superhuman speed and arachnid reflexes are not going to help with this one."

Dr. Banning stood up next, already looking a little green around the edges. "I'll rip the bastard limb from limb," he growled. His chest expanded, snapping the top three buttons off his shirt.

"Uh, I surely do appreciate the offer, Doctor, but I'm afraid superhuman anger is not the answer, either."

The Captain held up one hand to stop the verbal onslaught coming at him from every corner of the room. "In fact, no physical superpower will solve this dilemma.

According to our latest intelligence, the computerized detonation device is so sensitive the slightest touch will set it off. We need someone with psychic skills to defuse it."

Clark looked up from his laptop to find every eye in the room trained on him. Psychic skills? Hot damn! That was his department. Finally, a chance to prove brains beat brawn any day of the week.

He pushed his glasses up the bridge of his nose. "I'll be honored to take on the assignment, Captain."

"That's good of you, Clark, but not quite good enough, I'm afraid."

"But sir—I can psychically defuse any computerized bomb. All I have to do is get within ten feet of it."

"Yes, well, that's just our problem. Lex Loser's lair is three hundred feet underground, and it's impenetrable."

Bruce Wynn rose to his feet and crossed his arms. "Nothing's impenetrable, Captain. I'll blast my way in."

"Oh right." Clark didn't even try to hide his sarcasm. "Blow up the bomb. That'll work."

A collective twitter swept through the room. The rich playboy's face turned scarlet as he turned on Clark. Luckily, looks couldn't kill, or Clark would have been writhing on the floor, gasping for air.

"So what do you suggest, Geek Man? That we should just beam over, like on that *Star Trek* crap you're always watching?"

Captain Marvelous cleared his throat. "Now, now, boys. Petty rivalry has never saved the day in the past and it's not going to start now. I'm not exaggerating when I say the situation is bleak and getting worse by the second. The bomb is set to detonate in two days, twenty-three hours..." He checked his watch. "...and sixteen minutes."

That quieted everyone down in a hurry.

"Unless we can come up with a plan of action," The Captain intoned, "life as we know it..."

will... cease... to... exist, Clark mentally typed into the meeting minutes.

Bingo! The dire warning buzz phrase set off a renewed wave of furious whispers.

Clark frowned as he considered the various superpowers currently claimed by HUFF personnel. There were the mundane powers of strength, speed, and flight, and the rarer ones of x-ray vision, magnetic levitation, conjuring destructive weather on a perfectly sunny day, and setting oneself on fire with no untoward consequences.

And then there was the superpower of teleportation, which was kinda like the transporter on *Star Trek*...

Clark blinked. Teleportation!

That was it! If Clark could beam into Lex Loser's hideout, he could defuse the bomb. Well, what do you know? For once in his life, Bruce the feeble-brained superjerk had come up with an intelligent suggestion.

Teleportation wasn't a common superhero skill. In fact, it was the rarest. Currently, no one in HUFF claimed it. The last teleporting superhero, The Disappearing Man, had died twenty-four years ago while trying to teleport onto a stolen nuclear submarine. The poor guy had accidentally materialized underwater and drowned.

That embarrassing incident was rarely spoken of at HUFF headquarters. But Clark, who tended to spend Friday nights playing *Five Degrees of Wikipedia*, enlivened by the occasional bout of recreational hacking, had recently uncovered a heretofore unknown detail of the Disappearing Man's life story.

Using his laptop for a launching pad, he shot his mind through the wireless link to the HUFF mainframe, racing along a complex web of pathways. He ricocheted into the database, plunging deep and located the snippet of information where he'd filed it for future study.

When it was on his screen, he stood and waved one arm at The Captain.

"Yes, Clark?"

Clark pushed his glasses up the bridge of his nose. "Sir, I believe I have our answer."

Thursday, 1:02 am

Two days, twenty-two hours, fifty-eight minutes, and counting...

When it's too late for dinner and too early for breakfast, the only possible meal is ice cream.

Blossom snagged a quart of mint chocolate chip from the freezer. The real gourmet put-inches-on-your-hips stuff, not some fat-free taste-free frozen yogurt crap. Tucking her feet beneath her on the couch, she hit the play button on the remote and settled in. The familiar intro crooned. She dug her spoon into the cold, sweet cream and sighed with pleasure.

Faster than a speeding bullet... More powerful than a locomotive...

She looked over at the aquarium. Lois and Jimmy, the twin goldfish she'd won at the MPI Spring Fair, waved their fins at her. As if to say "get a life, girlfriend."

Able to leap tall buildings in a single bound...

Okay, maybe it was pathetic to spend the wee hours of the morning curled up on the couch watching 1950s Superman TV episodes, but hey, everyone had to have a hobby, right?

Look, there in the sky... It's a bird... It's a plane...

Blossom spooned the ice cream into her mouth and let it melt on her tongue. Aaaah.

It's Superman!

The episode was one of her favorites—#24, *Crime Wave*, in which Superman fights a mysterious rash of crime sweeping Metropolis, only to be nearly done in by atomic rays. So it was a bit—okay, a lot—corny, but satisfying nonetheless. Superman rocked.

His image graced her wall in an endless variety of poses, via the actors lucky enough to portray the Man of Steel in TV and film. From George Reeves to Henry Cavill, she lusted after them all. Superman's chiseled jaw, bulging biceps, and cute forehead curl greeted her at every turn. Superman comic books, vintage and modern, were stacked on every surface, amid lamps, lunchboxes and pillows. She'd spent literally thousands of dollars on Superman collectibles.

She refused to apologize! Even though some people— okay, most people—would call her unhealthily obsessed with a fictional character. So what if she had to eat spaghetti every night for a month to afford her latest eBay purchase?

When a girl spent her life surrounded by geeks, she did what she could to survive.

Thursday, 1:32 am

Two days, twenty-two hours, twenty-eight minutes, and counting...

"She's what?" Captain Marvelous asked.

"Half-human, half-superheroine," Clark explained patiently.

"Then why don't we know about her?" Bruce demanded. "Every superhero offspring is supposed to be evaluated for superpowers at puberty."

"Well, usually that's true, but this is a special case," Clark said. "Blossom Breeze was born after The Disappearing Man's fatal accident. With all the confusion and embarrassment following that event, no one even thought to ask his human wife if she was pregnant. Apparently Blossom's mother blamed HUFF for her husband's death, and she wasn't thrilled with the idea of having us involved with her daughter. At any rate, she disappeared soon after The Disappearing Man's funeral, and never registered her infant with headquarters. I stumbled across Blossom's birth records a few months ago, when I hacked into Megalopolis General during the Dr. Squid incident. I hunted around a bit further after the threat was neutralized. I accessed Blossom's medical and school records, took a look at her online presence, that sort of thing. I meant to bring the issue up at one of our regular monthly meetings, but we've been so busy lately, I forgot."

"You forgot," Bruce sneered. "Isn't that special. What if I'd forgotten to stop city bus #64 from plowing into that Girl Scout troop last week?"

The Captain shot Bruce a quelling look. "Are you sure The Disappearing Man is Blossom's father?" he asked Clark.

"Positive," Clark said. "She was conceived before his death, and his name is on her birth certificate. Her blood type's a match, too. If she's inherited his teleportation powers, it'd be a snap for her to get me into Lex's lair in time to defuse the bomb."

He called up Blossom Facebook profile pic. Bruce, Diana, and The Captain all crowded around the laptop for a better look.

"Not bad," said Bruce, letting a low whistle past his perfect teeth. "Not bad at all."

Diana elbowed him in the side.

"But not my type," he added hastily. "Too girl next door."

Clark enlarged the picture to full screen. "Girl next door" described Blossom perfectly. He wouldn't precisely describe her as beautiful. But she was cute, with short red hair and lots of freckles dancing across her nose. Her lips quirked, as if smiling at some secret joke. He found himself wondering if she was as fun to be with as she looked.

Diana flipped a strand of long, bouncy hair over one

bare shoulder. "She's twenty-four years old. Superpowers appear at puberty. If she could teleport, wouldn't there be evidence of it in her records?"

"Not necessarily," Clark said. "Her mother, who died several years ago, may have turned her against us. Or maybe Blossom doesn't even know about HUFF. She may have decided to keep her talent to herself, or maybe she doesn't even realize the extent of her powers. She's been living a mundane human life. She's a computer science grad student at Megalopolis Polytech."

"We must investigate this girl at once," declared Captain Marvelous. "The fate of the world depends upon it." He scanned the room. "I'll need a HUFF operative to travel to Megalopolis to assess the situation."

Of course, Bruce volunteered first. "I'll do it."

Like hell he would. Clark'd been itching for an excuse to get out of Newark for months. He sent another glance toward Blossom's picture. No way was he going to let Bruce muscle in on this assignment.

"This one's mine," he said quietly. "After all, Lex Loser is my nemesis."

Bruce started to protest, but The Captain held up one hand.

"I agree Clark's the hero for the job, Bruce, and not only because of Lex. Blossom Breeze, despite her parentage, is living an average life as an average human woman. She could very well faint dead away if a magnificent, larger-than-life superhero showed up on her doorstep." The Captain stroked the cleft in his chiseled chin.

"But Clark should do just fine."

Thursday, 2:46 pm
Two days, nine hours, fourteen minutes, and counting...

"Mind if I sit here?"

Blossom looked up from her book, only to find that the geeks of Megalopolis were not confined to the boundaries of the MPI computer lab. Apparently, they frequented the library, too. Geez. Where'd this guy get his black horn-rimmed glasses—the family planning aisle of the drug store? She was pretty sure their effectiveness as birth control surpassed The Pill.

"Suit yourself," she said, and returned to her book, *The Science of Superheroes.*

The geek set his laptop case on the floor and took the seat across the table from her. He opened a large tome and started reading. Blossom turned her shoulder a little, in case he got any ideas about talking to her. It wasn't vanity on her part. The guy had to be an idiot. Or a creeper. His book, *An Annotated History of Welding*, was upside down.

Unfortunately, her subtle hint didn't work. She wasn't entirely surprised. In her experience, subtle never worked with geeks.

"That looks like an interesting book," he ventured.

"Hmm." She turned a little more, taking *The Science of Superheroes* with her.

"Is there any special reason why you're reading it?"

She looked over at him. "I like superheroes."

For some reason, that seemed to encourage him. "Do you believe they're real?" His dark eyes regarded her seriously from behind Coke bottle lenses. Though he probably wouldn't look too bad if he got contacts, she decided.

"Do you?" he said again.

"Do I what?"

"Think superheroes are real?"

"Yeah, right," she said, and went back to reading.

The geek slipped off his chair, rounded the table, and took the seat to her right. Someone, she thought, should really tell him that the top button on a button down shirt was meant to be left open. Not her, though.

"I mean it," he said, drawing her attention back to him with a low, rich voice that seemed totally at odds with his persona. She closed her eyes and let it wash over her.

"Did you ever imagine what it would be like if superheroes really existed?" he asked.

Did she ever. She thought about it every night in bed. But those kinds of thoughts weren't something a girl shared with a sort of cute, geeky stranger. Or even with a best girlfriend, for that matter.

"I guess there'd be less crime," she said finally.

"Maybe there *is* less crime."

Huh? "What's that supposed to mean?"

He took a deep breath. A springy lock of dark hair fell onto his forehead.

Very cute, she thought. Then she remembered the

laptop. *Very geeky.*

"Maybe," he said, "there would be more crime if there weren't superheroes."

Say again? "Yeah," she said. "Maybe." *Not.*

"I bet you've always felt different from other people," he said.

She gave him her best frown. What was this guy talking about? He looked harmless enough, but... She scooted her chair a couple inches back from the table, just in case she had to make a run for it.

"It can be frightening to discover you have a superpower. Especially if you're just a teenager, and there's no one around to guide you."

Yep. Certifiable. Did she know how to attract them, or what? She closed *The Science of Superheroes* with a thud.

"Oh, would you look at the time," she exclaimed, flashing her cell phone. "I've really got to go. Right away. I've got an appointment."

His hand settled on her arm. "You don't have to pretend with me, Blossom."

She jumped back, nearly knocking her chair over in her haste. "You know my name?" she all but screeched. "What are you, some crazy stalker?"

The librarian glared.

"No, nothing like that," he said. "I just—"

She flattened her palms on the table and leaned across. "Look," she whispered furiously, "I don't know who you are or what you think you know about me, but I'm warning you. Stay away from me or I'm calling the cops."

Thursday, 2:55 pm
Two days, nine hours, five minutes, and counting...

Well. That didn't go over quite the way he'd planned.

Clark morosely contemplated the door through which Blossom Breeze had fled. *Smooth one, Geek Man.* He gave a heavy sigh. Either Blossom was hiding her superpower, or her human genes had proved dominant and she was just your everyday, average, appealing-as-all-hell woman.

He let his mind wander a bit on that one. Blossom didn't have Diana's curves or cup size, but when she'd blinked up at him with those big blue eyes he'd felt it like a sucker punch to the gut. He'd experienced a sudden urge to sift his fingers through her sassy red hair and plant a kiss on her lush pink lips.

She said she liked superheroes, right?

Well, *he* was a superhero, wasn't he?

Of course, she'd never guess it. Which was exactly why The Captain had sent him on this mission. A mission he might have already blown with his bungling attempt at first contact. Clark gave an inward groan. *Bruce* wouldn't have crashed and burned. *Bruce* would've come up with a suave opening line. *Bruce* would've been on his way home with Blossom right now.

He stared at her vacated chair. Something caught his eye, and he leaned forward. A single strand of red hair clung to the chair's upholstered back. He lifted it carefully. This specimen was just what he needed to determine whether his trip to Megalopolis was humanity's best hope for survival or a complete waste of time.

Returning to his original seat, he shoved *An Annotated History of Welding* to one side and hefted his laptop case onto the desk. In a few moments, he'd powered up his computer and enabled the genetic testing program. He attached the sensor wand—his own invention--to the USB port. He ran the tip over Blossom's fiery strand of hair.

The string of genetic code scrolled up the screen faster than a normal human eye could register. Clark, however, had no trouble following the analysis. As the lines of coded numbers streamed by, his excitement built. His analysis showed that Blossom's super genes were no match for her human mother's contribution to her DNA.

She was most definitely a superheroine.

Yes!

"Young man, keep it down!" The librarian looked ready to kill.

Clark gave her a guilty glance. Had he shouted out loud? "Yes, Ma'am." He took a calming breath and sank his mind into the readout file.

Wait one minute. Something wasn't quite right. Yes, Blossom carried the gene for teleportation, but for some reason it wasn't epigenetically active. Which meant that the gene hadn't switched on at puberty. Which meant that currently, she couldn't change locations with a thought, taking whomever she touched with her. Which meant that she wasn't going to be able to teleport Clark into Lex's underground lair.

Stomach churning, Clark launched another sequence of programs, further refining his genetic investigation.

Two-point-seven minutes later, he broke out in a cold sweat. According to his expanded analysis, Blossom carried a rare genetic mutation. The variation had prevented her superpower gene from switching on with the first influx of puberty hormones, as was typical with most super-offspring. In Blossom's case, it looked like a different, more specialized hormone surge was needed to trigger the gene's epigenetic activity.

A bead of sweat broke out on Clark's brow. Was it hot in here? He checked the time. Noon. *Two days, eight hours, seventeen minutes and thirty-nine seconds to go.* As little as he wanted to, he should really check in with these latest findings. After a brief hesitation, he sighed and opened a Velcro pocket on his laptop case. He pulled out his cell and tapped in The Captain's private number.

"Well, what's the word, Clark? Don't spare the details. Can humanity be saved?"

Briefly, Clark summarized his unexpected discovery. "All we have to do is initiate the specialized hormone flux and Blossom's superpower gene will switch on," he concluded. "When that happens, she'll have full translocation powers."

"And just how do we do that, son?"

The library was definitely getting uncomfortably warm. Probably a malfunction in the air handling system. Clark inserted his index finger into the collar of his shirt and tugged it away from his heated skin. "Well, Captain, the thing is... I mean, the only way this precise combination of hormones can be released is...um..."

Upon which point Clark's courage deserted him completely.

Some superhero, he thought.

"Go on, Clark, and be quick about it. We haven't got all day, you know."

He took a deep breath and tried again. "I'm sorry, sir. I know we don't. Okay. It's like this. The only way to trigger the transformation is for Blossom... uh, I mean Ms. Breeze, to..." He swallowed hard.

"Spit it out, boy!"

His face flamed. Closing his eyes, he let the words spill. "The only way for Blossom to access her superheroine talent isforhertohavea—" He caught his breath. Opening one eye, he glanced toward the librarian.

The woman folded her arms across her chest and gave him back a glare.

Half turning in his seat, he cupped a hand around the phone and dropped his voice. "She needs to have a sexual encounter, Captain. But not just any sexual encounter. She has to...um...*finish*, if you catch my meaning, sir. In a big way. According to my calculation, it has to be a full-tilt, off-the-charts happy ending. In short, in order for the gene to switch on, Blossom Breeze has to experience toe-curling, mind-blowing, deep-muscle-contracting sexual ecstasy."

With a gulp, Clark fell silent. A full ten seconds passed, in which nothing but dead silence poured through the cell phone waves.

Then Captain Marvelous, recovering, cleared his throat.

"Clark," he barked, "the fate of humanity is at stake. What in blue blazes are you waiting for? Get right on it."

Friday, 5:29 am

One day, eighteen hours, thirty-one minutes, and counting...

Blossom shielded her eyes from the rising sun as she scurried from the MPI Math Center to her ancient Volkswagen Jetta. Another all-nighter—unfortunately, one that hadn't included a single alcoholic beverage or grope in the dark with a muscle-bound stranger. She slung her backpack off her shoulder and fished around in it for her car keys.

Lois and Jimmy were right. She was pathetic.

"Hey," a deep voice said, right in her ear.

She nearly jumped a mile.

It was the crazy geek from the library, dressed in another short sleeve button-up-to-the-neck shirt—*plaid*, no less. His black pants showed at least two inches of knobby ankle. As if to complete this object study of pure geekiness, he held an enormous laptop case in one hand.

"You again! Can't you take a hint?"

"Apparently not," he said wryly.

She opened her mouth to chew him out, then stopped. Something about him made her not want to shoot him. Maybe it was that cute half-of-a-shy-smile he was directing her way. She'd hate to kill something that endearing.

"Geez," she said instead. "You startled me."

"Sorry. I didn't mean to."

"Oh, well, no problem," she told him. "I love being scared out of my wits. The adrenaline rush will help get me home without falling asleep."

The half smile became a full one. "Up all night?"

"Yeah. Had a bug it took a while to find."

"I get like that, too," he said. "Time flies when you're coding." He plucked the keys from her hand. Before Blossom realized what was happening, he'd guided her around to the passenger's side, unlocked the door, and helped her in.

"Wait a minute," she said. "What do you think you're doing?"

"You're dead on your feet. I can't let you drive home."

"That's the worst pick up line I've ever heard," she told him. She climbed back out of the car. "Do you really think I'm gonna let some stranger drive me home? For all I know, you could be an ax murderer."

"Do I look dangerous enough?" His eyes seemed hopeful.

"Looks aren't everything," Blossom said.

"True," he said, his smile widening. "But in my case you really have nothing to worry about. I'd never hurt you."

He was kind of cute when he smiled. But... "I don't know," she said. "You have to admit, you were a little over the top at the library yesterday. All that talk of superheroes being real—"

"A joke," he said quickly. "I have a... um... unique

sense of humor." He dangled the keys. "I'll just drive you home. No funny stuff. I promise."

"No. Give me back my keys."

"Forget it. If you won't let me drive, I'm calling a cab."

"You don't have to do that."

"I know." He un-Velcroed a pocket on his laptop case and dug out a cell phone.

Twenty minutes later, the cab still hadn't come. "Megalopolis cab service sucks," he grumbled.

"I could've told you that," Blossom said, yawning. "*Now* can I have my keys back? I really need to get some sleep."

He sighed. "All right. But I'm going to follow you home. Just to make sure you get there okay."

Great. Just great.

"One-sixteen Oakland, right?" he asked, handing the keys over.

She froze. "How did you know that?"

"Your backpack," he said, pointing.

Yep, there it was. Right on the tag, under her name, for any and all potential perverts to see. Lovely. She might as well have recorded her bra size, too.

She glared at him. He grinned back.

"Who are you?" she asked irritably. "And why are you following me around?"

He held out his hand. "Dr. Clark Kendall. I'm... new at MPI. I'm here for a special research project."

She stared at him for a beat, then started to laugh. "That's good," she said. "A bit corny, but good."

"What?"

"Your name. Clark Kendall. Almost like Superman."

"Yeah," he said. "Almost."

She got in the car and grabbed the inside door handle. He leaned in, one hand on the roof and the other on the window frame, keeping her from shutting the door. "Listen," he said. "After I tail you home and you catch up on your sleep, how about going out to dinner with me?"

"You don't give up easy, do you?"

He smiled again, a big, lopsided grin that showed a dimple in each cheek. A thick, curling shank of dark hair fell across his forehead. She stared at it, mesmerized. Wow. *Just like Super—*

No. That was crazy talk. Man, she needed some sleep. She looked up, trying to see his eyes, but with the sun striking just so on his glasses, all she could see was her own reflection.

"Come on," he pressed. "I'll take you to that fancy Italian restaurant over on Broad Street. What's it called?"

"Luigi's," she said. "But you're kidding, right? That place is five star. It'll cost you a fortune."

"You're worth it."

"Why?" she asked. "Why are you doing this? You don't even know me."

He shrugged and looked away.

"You're really a visiting prof?" she asked. "What's your research about?"

"Genetics," he said after a slight pause. "Epigenetic hormone triggers in dominant and recessive DNA combinations."

"Wow," she said. "Sounds wild."

"You have no idea. So what do you say? Have dinner with me tonight?"

She hesitated, then sighed. Truth was, she loved authentic Italian food. She'd been dying to go to Luigi's ever since it opened last semester, but with no significant other in sight, and every spare dime spent on Superman memorabilia, she hadn't quite managed to get there. She might as well go with Dr. Clark Kendall. He was a geek, but hey, it wasn't like the real Clark Kent was going to show up at her door any time soon.

"All right," she said.

"Come on, you need to eat anyw— Wait. What did you say?"

She laughed. "I said all right."

He looked stunned. "Really?"

She considered his short sleeved, buttoned-up shirt, and his where's-the-flood khakis. Second thoughts—heck, third and fourth and fifth thoughts, too—crowded her brain.

"On one condition," she said.

He pushed his glasses up the bridge of his nose. "What's that?"

"Lose the geek clothes."

Friday, 1:06 pm
One day, ten hours, fifty-four minutes, and counting...

Lose the geek clothes.

Right. No problem. He could do that.

Clark stared at the rack of MegaMart polyester dress suits and heaved a sigh. Give him an FBI mainframe to hack into, no prob-lemmo. Tell him to dress up for a dinner date, and he was up shit creek without a toilet brush for a paddle.

What would Bruce wear? He winced. Now wouldn't *that* make a good bumper sticker.

"Need some help, hon?"

He turned to find a fifty-something, big-haired, gum-snapping saleslady hovering at his elbow. The woman outweighed him by a good seventy pounds. He squinted at her name tag. *Janey.*

He stepped back so quickly, he nearly fell over his laptop case. "I'm not sure."

"Well, then, honey, I'm your dream come true. I know all there is to know about dressing men." She gave him a once over. "Undressing 'em, too."

"Is that so?" Clark asked faintly.

"Damn straight. Got seven boys of my own, you know. From five different papas."

"That's...amazing."

She cocked her head to one side. "What you getting all slicked up for?"

"A dinner date," he told her. "At Luigi's."

Janey pursed her fire-alarm red lips and whistled. "Ooooh. Fancy shmancy. You'll need the works."

"What do you suggest?" Clark asked, not at all sure he wanted to know, but seeing no way to politely back out of the conversation.

"I like the Seventies look, myself." She clamped a hand around his upper arm and towed him toward a discount sign. "Takes me right back to high school." She fished through the rack and reeled in a blinding white suit, with lapels wider than Clark's hand. She flung the pants and jacket over one substantial shoulder, then womanhandled Clark over to the shirts, where she slithered a slippery black one off a hanger.

He guessed the material was supposed to look like silk, but a glance at the price tag told him the garment was pure petroleum by-products.

"I'm not sure I—"

"Sure you are," Janey said, shoving him into the dressing room. "Remember Saturday Night Fever?"

"No, actually I've never seen—"

The louvered door slammed. "Get dressed now, hon."

"But—"

"Honey, you want me to come in there and dress you myself?"

That threat was enough to scare Clark right out of his boxers. With a sigh, he set down his laptop case and got to work. He emerged a few minutes later, shaking his head.

"I don't know..." He peered into the full length mirror and grimaced. "Are bellbottoms really back in style?"

"Honey," Janey said, surveying him up and down, "no way am I letting you slide those skinny legs of yours into a pair of them tight ankle nancy pants all the boys are wearing these days. What you need is volume, my little man. What you got on is just the thing. Your girl's gonna drag you off into the first empty corner and jump your bones."

She draped a heavy gold chain around his neck and pinched his cheek. "Trust me."

Friday, 6:41 pm
One day, five hours, nineteen minutes, and counting...

Perhaps his trust had been a little misplaced, Clark thought as he tried to catch Blossom's gaze across the intimate table for two at Luigi's. His date didn't seem too taken with his new clothes. Her gaze kept roaming, as if it hurt to look at him.

She, on the other hand, looked great. She was wearing a sleek, rust colored, off-the-shoulder dress. It dipped a bit in the front, showing the slightest bit of cleavage. Classy, not flashy.

Clark tugged at the collar of his faux silk shirt. The restaurant was kind of warm. What was it with the air conditioners in this town?

Then again, maybe it was just nerves. He wished he'd had a few days to ease into this assignment—feel his way around, so to speak. But he didn't. Lex Loser's bomb was set to go off—he discreetly checked his cell phone—in twenty-nine hours, seventeen minutes, and six seconds. It was do or die, *Geek Man*.

Literally.

"How's your ossobucco?" he ventured.

Blossom's gaze focused on his face. "What? Oh, fine. Very good. How's your calamari?"

He gulped down some pinot grigio. "Um… Interesting, I guess."

"You've never had it before?"

"No." And he'd ordered it without reading the fine print translation on the menu. *Squid.* Ugh.

Manfully, he forked another dangling, suction-cupped tentacle into his mouth. He swallowed without chewing, then washed the whole disgusting mess down his gullet with another healthy swig of fine wine. Damn if it wasn't getting hotter in here by the minute. And he had an itch on his ankle. Surreptitiously, he inched his foot to one side until it came into contact with his laptop case. He rubbed it up and down. The relief was fleeting.

"So how long are you in town for?" Blossom asked.

"Uh, not too long," Clark said.

"Where do you usually live?"

"Newark, New Jersey."

"Oh."

And if the conversation had gone downhill from there, at least it hadn't had far to fall, Clark reflected as he walked Blossom home. Trouble was, he'd never in his life asked a woman out with the explicit goal of getting her into bed. Well, not on the first date, at least. It just didn't seem respectful. He believed in the getting-to-know-you stage. Which led to the falling-in-love stage. Which led to the hot monkey sex stage.

Not that he'd ever had hot monkey sex personally, but he'd seen videos of it on the Internet. He was more than willing to give it a try with Blossom, if she seemed at all interested. He sidled a glance in her direction. She was walking a step in front of him, her head up, high heels clicking on the sidewalk. Her cute round bottom swayed back and forth. The sight made him slightly dizzy.

Don't panic, he told himself. He could do this. He had to. After all, the fate of the world hung in the balance. He was going to make his move. Right now.

They reached Blossom's apartment door. "Can I come in?" Clark asked, shifting his laptop case from his right hand to his left. "For, um, a glass of water? I'm kinda thirsty."

Ah, hell. Another smooth line. Wasn't he just full of them tonight? He wasn't kidding about the water, though. He was parched. And damn if his back didn't itch like nobody's business. He shifted his shoulders, trying to get some relief without being too obvious.

Blossom hesitated. "Well, okay. Just for a minute."

She fished her house key from her purse. It dangled from a Superman key chain.

Cool, Clark thought. He rocked back on his heels as she unlocked the door, then followed her over the threshold. She flicked the light switch.

He blinked, sure his eyes were playing tricks on him. He put down the laptop, took off his glasses, checked them for smudges, and put them back on again. No, he wasn't hallucinating. The keychain was the least of it.

Blossom's apartment was a veritable shrine to Superman.

Every square millimeter of wall space was dedicated to

the Man of Steel, in all his various comic, TV, and movie incarnations. Vintage comic books, professionally framed and mounted, hung above the sofa. Posters of George Reeve, Dean Cain, Christopher Reeves, and Tom Welling marched along the opposite wall. A Superman lunchbox perched on a shelf in the kitchen. A revolving Daily Planet desk lamp adorned the table near the door. A movie poster from the most recent reboot, autographed by Henry Cavill himself, was propped against a side table.

Incredible.

"You got a thing for Superman?" he asked.

"Yeah," she said, giving him a sheepish grin. "Pretty weird, huh?"

"Not at all," Clark said quickly. "I think it's great. I'm a Superman fan myself."

"You are?"

"Yeah. Because of my name." He resisted scratching a fierce itch on the inside of his elbow. "I collect Superman comic books, mostly. I have a complete set of Golden Age Action Comics from 1947 through 1956." He frowned. "Well, except for #158. I tried to buy that one on eBay Wednesday night, but someone snatched it right out from under my nose."

Blossom's blue eyes went round. "*You're* the one who ran up that bid? You jerk! You cost me five hundred dollars!"

She was his mystery bidder? "You didn't have to go so high," Clark protested. "You could've dropped out and let me have it."

"No way was I going to fold! I've been looking for that issue for a solid year."

"So have I," Clark said, then laughed. "But if I had to lose it, I'm glad it was to you."

Blossom smiled. "Really?"

"Yes," said Clark, resisting the urge to claw the niggling itch on his thigh. He moved close, daring to brush his fingers over the freckles on Blossom's cheek. She didn't move away. His heart tripped up a beat, then resumed in double time.

He started to sweat. For as many times as he'd envisioned this moment, you would think that he'd have come up with some sort of plan. Instead, he was clueless. Should he try to kiss her now? God, it was hot in here. Another malfunctioning air conditioner? Must be an epidemic.

His gaze dropped to her lips. They were full and lush, a little pouty. Sweat trickled down behind his collar. A new itch hit him on the neck. He ignored everything and leaned closer, until their lips were only inches apart.

Her eyes fluttered closed.

Was it his imagination, or was she swaying toward him? Emboldened, he framed her face in his hands, threaded his fingers through her hair. His heart beat so loudly it sounded like a New Age drum circle had invaded his rib cage.

Their lips touched. Clark felt the contact from his mouth down to his toes, and in a few strategic places in between. He angled his head a little, to get his glasses out of the way of the kiss. He really should have thought to take them off earlier.

Blossom trembled a bit. Her hands came to rest on his arms. His thigh itched again, distracting him. He shook off the intrusion and kissed her again, a little harder and longer this time.

Was it too early for tongues?

Maybe, but he really didn't have time to waste. He decided to go for it.

He wrapped Blossom in his arms, urging her closer as he stroked her lower lip with the tip of his tongue. She sighed, opening her mouth and going all soft in his arms. An invitation? He hoped so. His tongue slid inside. Stroked in and out.

Oh, yeah. This was it. His little Man of Steel was *so* ready to save the world.

But the back of his neck itched like hell.

He moved one hand around Blossom's torso, into breast territory. Easy... Easy... He didn't want to scare her. After all, he knew for a fact she'd never had a memorable sexual experience. She was probably shy about things like this.

His fingers found their goal. Closed on soft, quivering flesh...

Blossom swatted his hand away. He tried an evasive maneuver. She attempted a block. He circumvented it.

She knocked him on his ass.

He lay flat on his back on the carpet, staring up at her. "Wha...?"

"Self-defense class." She looked startled, yet satisfied. "You know, I never thought that move would really work."

"Geez. From where I'm lying, looks like it worked fine."

"Well, you deserved it," she declared, arms akimbo. "Trying to cop a feel on a first date. You should be ashamed of yourself."

He sat up, rubbing the back of his head. "Sorry."

Blossom pointed toward the door. "Out."

"Hey," he said, jumping to his feet. "Don't you think that's a little hasty?"

"No," she said. "I mean, it's not like I'm going to see you again or anything."

"Not see me—" Hell, that didn't sound at all encouraging. He wriggled to evade a sudden itch on his hip. "Why not? I thought we were getting along great."

"We were," Blossom said, "but that's not the point."

Even if he lived out the average superhero lifespan of two hundred and three, Clark would never, ever get the hang of female logic. "All right. I'll bite. What is the point?"

"The point is you look like John Travolta's scrawny little brother. I couldn't possibly go out with you again."

"I don't even like this outfit," Clark protested, ignoring her slander of his physique. "The saleslady picked it out."

"And you let her? That's even worse. Look, I spend all day and most nights surrounded by geeks. No offense, but I don't think I can go twenty-four seven with it. It's too hard on the eyes."

Clark scanned the collage of superhero muscle on her walls, his heart sinking. He had a pretty good idea what

Blossom was looking for in a lover. No matter how you sliced and diced it, he didn't have what she wanted.

Still, he couldn't give up. Not with Lex's bomb set to blow.

He tried to reason with her. "Looks aren't everything. Didn't you say that yesterday?"

"Did I?" Blossom said. "I must have been out of my mind. Looks are huge. Ninety percent of the information humans receive from their environment is visual. For me it's probably more like a hundred and one percent." She sighed. "Look, I'm sorry, Clark. I just can't help how I am. You're a great guy and all, but—"

But. Clark hated when a woman said that word. In his experience it was usually followed by...

"—can't we just be friends?"

"Of course," he said, going for his standard reply.

The itch on his neck grew unbearable. Weighted down by Blossom's rejection, he finally cracked. He gave in and scratched.

The prickle darted to his solar plexus. His fingers followed it. After that, it split, attacking both shoulders at once. Then it reached flashpoint, racing across his chest, down his arms and legs, up over his face...

"Are you okay?" Blossom asked. "Because, you know, you don't look so good."

Clark dropped to his knees, knocking over his laptop case on the way down. He tried desperately to reach a spot right in the middle of his back. But the itching was the least of his problems. It was getting hard to breathe. Little red spots swirled into his vision.

"Call 911," he gasped, just before he blacked out.

Friday, 11:22 pm
One day, thirty-eight minutes, and counting...

"Hives and anaphylaxis," Clark told Blossom when he emerged from the emergency room, looking beat. "The doctor thinks it was the calamari."

She jumped to her feet. "You scared me half to death! I'm still shaking. You could have died."

"Look on the bright side," Clark said. "If I get bored tonight, I can play dot to dot on my chest."

She giggled. Then sobered as her gaze dropped. The top two buttons on Clark's shirt were, for once, unbuttoned. Angry red welts covered his skin, looking horribly uncomfortable.

"Does it itch very badly?" she asked.

He grimaced. "Bad enough."

She clucked in sympathy, and looked at his chest some more. It might not be superhero material, but it wasn't really *that* scrawny. Suddenly, she felt a little ashamed at how she'd treated him during their date.

"I'm sorry about what I said earlier," she told him.

"Which time?" he asked. But he was smiling when he said it. He had a nice smile. And he was so at ease poking fun at himself. There was something very appealing about that.

"When I said you were scrawny," she said.

"Oh, that." He glanced down at his chest. "No apology needed for the truth." He caught her gaze and held it. "I'm the one who should be apologizing. My behavior was less than gentlemanly."

"Forget about it," Blossom said, coloring. "No offense taken." The truth was, she'd enjoyed kissing Clark. Too much. That, more than anything else, had caused her to back off. She just couldn't bear the thought of a geek boyfriend.

"The doctor gave me a shot," Clark was saying. "It'll take a few hours to work." He gave a half laugh. "I don't think I'll get much sleep tonight."

"I'm a night owl myself," Blossom said. "You know...maybe..." She stopped herself, suddenly uncertain.

He stilled, an arrested look on his face. "Maybe what?"

Why did it seem so hard to breathe all of a sudden? *Just friends,* she reminded herself. "As long as we're both going to be up anyway, I was thinking maybe you'd like to come back to my place. We could stay up together. And maybe we could even..."

She hesitated. No guy she'd ever dated had wanted to do what she was about to propose. Would Clark be shocked? Dismayed? Worse, would he laugh?

Well, there was only one way to find out. She drew a deep breath.

"...maybe we could even watch some 1950s Superman TV episodes? I have a pretty big collection on DVD."

"Cool," Clark said without missing a beat. "Do you

have the one where an asteroid gives Superman amnesia?"

Blossom's heart gave a funny little jump. "Episode #38. Panic in the Sky. Yep, I have it."

"Great," said Clark. "That's my favorite."

Saturday, 5:59 am
Eighteen hours, one minute, and counting...

Clark woke up slowly, every muscle protesting. Somehow he'd twisted himself into a pretzel on a couch that was way too soft to offer much support to his back. He blinked up at the wall and frowned at the four color hammered tin image of a vintage Superman, chest muscles bulging as he tore apart a heavy chain with his bare hands.

Where the hell was he?

Oh yeah. Blossom's living room.

They'd had a great night, despite the residual itching from the calamari. They'd watched episode after episode of classic Superman, laughing over the cheesy special effects, but loving the stories all the same. Blossom had changed from her dress into a comfortable oversized tee-shirt and men's boxers. She'd made popcorn, and poured soda, and they stayed up until four am.

But he hadn't touched her once.

Groaning, Clark rolled over and eyed the door to her bedroom. The firmly closed door to her bedroom. Bruce would have been in there by now, he reflected bleakly. Bruce's physique would have blinded Blossom to his less-than-superheroic emotional traits, providing him quick and easy access to her bed. And once there, Bruce would have wasted no time in plying his legendary bedroom skills to give Blossom the sexual fulfillment she needed to trigger her own powers.

Still, things could be worse. At least he and Blossom shared the basics for a good friendship. They liked the same jokes, and she loved superheroes and everything about them. Plus, she seemed to be comfortable around him.

He grimaced. As long as she didn't look at him, that is. But he *had* spent the night at her apartment. She could have kicked him out, but she hadn't. That counted for something, right? Given enough time...

Except he didn't have enough time.

Shit.

He should have been expecting Captain Marvelous' wake-up call, but his ringtone still took him by surprise.

He grabbed his glasses with one hand and his laptop case with the other. He tore open the Velcro and pulled out his cell. "Kendall here."

"What's the report, Clark? Are you in yet?"

Clark winced at The Captain's choice of words. "Uh, not exactly, sir."

"Not good enough, Clark, you know that. Time's running out."

Clark gave a surreptitious glance toward Blossom's door. "I'm working on it. I spent the night in her apartment."

The Captain perked up. "In her bedroom?"

"Uh, no," Clark said. "On the couch."

A brief silence ensued, then The Captain heaved a sigh. "Clark, much as I hate to admit it, I'm beginning to think I made a mistake sending you to Megalopolis."

Clark struggled to right himself on the understuffed couch cushion. "Not at all, Captain. I can do this. I just need a little more time."

"Unfortunately, that's something I don't have to give," The Captain said. "Lex's bomb is set to go off in…"

"…seventeen hours, fifty-eight minutes, and three seconds," Clark finished for him. "Believe me, I know."

"Then you understand I've got no choice, son. I'm sending in backup."

Clark's stomach abruptly knotted. "Who?"

"Why, Bruce Wynn, of course. Who else?"

Saturday, 6:15 am
Seventeen hours, forty-five minutes, and counting...

Blossom was dressing when she heard Clark's phone ring. Who would call him at this hour?

A girlfriend?

The thought made her stomach lurch, though she couldn't quite imagine why. It's not like she wanted him for herself or anything. Even though she'd had more fun last night in... heck, she didn't know how long. Clark was really the nicest guy. She revised her theory about the girlfriend caller. It just didn't seem in Clark's character to cheat on an unsuspecting significant other. Not that any cheating had gone on, mind you. The whole night had been totally innocent.

Blossom zipped up her jeans and wriggled into a green and gold MPI tee-shirt. She and Clark had watched TV for hours, but he hadn't tried to kiss her again. She felt a little conflicted about that. On one hand, he'd had plenty of opportunity. She should be insulted he hadn't taken advantage of it. On the other hand, who could blame him if he hadn't? When he'd tried it the first time, she'd decked him.

She eased open the door. "Clark? Are you up?" She wouldn't want him to think she was eavesdropping.

He shoved his phone into his laptop case. "Yeah," he

said, getting to his feet.

His white pants were a bit rumpled, but at least his black shirt was all the way unbuttoned now, and hanging loose. His feet were bare. Somehow, that seemed unsettling.

She made it halfway across the room before her legs refused to take her any further. "Your chest looks a lot better," she said. Inanely. "I mean, the hives and all."

"The itching's gone," he replied, not moving.

She changed direction, heading for the kitchen. "Want some coffee? I usually pick it up on my way to the lab, but I can—"

"No thanks," he said. "Let's go out to breakfast."

"Can't. I have a meeting with my advisor at seven."

"On a Saturday morning?"

"Yeah. Grad students don't exactly keep corporate hours."

"Meet me after, then."

"I have a ton of work to do."

His tone turned desperate. "Lunch, then. You have to eat, right?"

"I guess. How 'bout the Sunrise Diner? It's a couple blocks down the street, on Main. At eleven forty-five?"

"It'll have to do," said Clark. "See you then."

Saturday, 8:48 am
Fifteen hours, twelve minutes, and counting...

Clark leaned on the stand up counter at the local coffeehouse and took a bracing gulp of his caramel latte. He had to do something about Blossom. The "just friends" thing was all very well and good, but with time ticking by like—well, like an armed computerized neutron bomb—he couldn't afford to kick back and await favorable developments. He had to come up with a viable plan for her seduction. Maybe one that would take Blossom's mind off her narrow visual focus and let her concentrate on her feelings? He knew she liked him a little. If she harbored even one one-hundredth of the attraction he felt for her, he would succeed.

After years of fantasizing about Diana Price, it was odd he should feel this way. Diana was every man's dream. She was centerfold-worthy. Tall. Voluptuous. Gorgeous. Self-confident. Hot enough to burn. If Diana had a brain, it wasn't immediately apparent. And, Clark had to admit, he'd never really cared. It wasn't as though he dreamed about discussing philosophy with her.

Blossom couldn't begin to compete with Diana. Sure, she was cute, especially with all those freckles on her upturned nose, but no one would hand her first place in the Miss Megalopolis contest. Her breasts were barely a B cup, and her legs weren't long and shapely. Her hair frizzed a little. But she was smart. And fun, once you got past that I-hate-geeks thing. She had a great sense of humor, and to Clark, that counted for a lot.

She was a little unsure of herself, in an endearing kind of way. Maybe that was why she obsessed so much about Superman. Maybe subconsciously, she wanted to set her standard so high no man could reach it. So she wouldn't get hurt.

I wouldn't hurt her, Clark thought. If she wanted him, he'd be hers in three nanoseconds flat. After he triggered Blossom's superpowers and saved the world, they could hook up for good. He took a long sip of coffee, spinning that fantasy for a while. They could get married, buy a house in the suburbs not too far from HUFF headquarters, have two-point-three kids and a dog...

But he had to get her into bed first, before Bruce arrived on the scene. Once Mr. Six-Pack showed up, Clark would be toast. Blossom would take one look at Bruce's steroid enhanced pectorals and melt into a gooey puddle on the sidewalk. And why shouldn't she? Every woman did.

A hot rush of anger surged through him. No way could he let Bruce Wynn, *Superjerk*, use and discard Blossom. Clark would face down a whole freezer full of calamari before he'd let that happen.

If only he could get Blossom's mind off the visual...

He straightened abruptly. That was it!

Get Blossom's mind off the visual.

Could he do it?

Saturday, 12:15 pm
Eleven hours, forty-five minutes, and counting...

Blossom dumped three packs of sugar into her iced tea, all the while keeping one eye on the door. Clark was late. He wouldn't stand her up, would he? A little twitch of fear wiggled in her stomach. Maybe he'd decided *she* was too geeky for *him*. He wouldn't be the first guy to decide that.

"Hey, babe. Got a minute?"

The speaker was a man. A beautiful man, standing right in front of her. Blossom looked over her shoulder, but she didn't see anyone else he might have been speaking to.

She turned back. "You mean me?"

"Yeah, babe. You."

She drank him in. Over six feet tall, with dark hair, dark eyes, and chiseled features. And dressed all in delicious black. A tee-shirt stretched so tight across his unbelievable chest it was in danger of coming apart at the seams. Leather pants hugged lean hips and long muscular legs with just the right amount of loving cling. Blossom's eyes widened. The incredible bulge between his thighs was definitely superhero material.

Her stomach executed an Olympic-grade backflip. This guy outshone every last poster on her wall. God, he was hot. Scorching. Just touching him would probably give her third degree burns.

"Did...did you want me for something?" she stuttered.

"Oh, yeah." He let the words hang there in the air between them until she blushed. "May I join you?"

"Me?" He had to be kidding. No man in his league had ever even blinked in her direction.

His gaze drifted over her, sending little tingles zapping all over her skin. "I saw you sitting here," he said. "And I thought, what a crime such a beautiful girl has to eat lunch alone. I'll buy you lunch, babe."

She stared at him for a good five seconds before she realized he was waiting for some kind of reply. "Um, sure?" She gave a feeble wave toward the empty booth seat opposite.

Oh, wait. What about Clark? She glanced toward the door. Well, heck. He was the one who was late. It would serve him right to find her with another man. Not that it mattered. After all, it wasn't as if she and Clark had anything going on.

She swallowed a little pang of guilt as the hottie's perfect butt slid across the vinyl bench seat.

She shoved a menu at him. "What would you like?"

He held her gaze. "I'm looking at it, babe."

"Oh," squeaked Blossom, her throat suddenly dry. She licked her lips. His incredible eyes darkened.

Oh, God.

"What did you say your name was?" she asked.

Saturday, 12:31 pm
Eleven hours, twenty-nine minutes, and counting...

The key to success in any venture, Clark decided as he hurried to his lunch date with Blossom, lay in careful research and meticulous planning. Of course, promptness didn't hurt either. He checked his watch and winced. He was late, late, late. He hoped Blossom didn't think he'd stood her up.

He clutched his laptop case in one hand, thinking of the extra items it now held. Items he'd purchased, then promptly hidden in the zippered and Velcroed pockets. The store he'd visited was the kind that didn't open until noon, and it had taken a little time—after he'd recovered from pure shock—to sort through its offerings. After all, the fate of the world depended on his choices.

He hurried the last few steps to the Sunrise Diner and shoved open the door.

And stopped dead in his tracks.

Shit.

Bruce Wynn was in the house.

Clark plowed through the knot of customers at the door. He'd known The Captain was sending Bruce to seduce Blossom, but the bald reality of the situation hadn't registered until now. His stomach lurched as Bruce's manicured hand crept across the table to stroke Blossom's fingers. He said something. Something idiotic, no doubt.

She blushed and giggled.

No way was this gonna happen, Clark thought darkly. Blossom was much too nice a girl to get snagged and snogged by a predator like Bruce. Clark pushed his glasses up the bridge of his nose and squared his shoulders. His grip tightened on the handle of his laptop case.

He marched to Blossom's rescue.

"Hello, Blossom," he said.

"Oh! Clark." She didn't quite meet his gaze.

"I thought we had a lunch date."

Bruce lounged back, one muscled arm draped over the back of the booth seat. An amused smile played on his lips.

Blossom's eyes sparked. "We did have a lunch date, Clark. The one that you're half an hour late for. Luckily, I got another invitation." She waved a hand across the table. "This is Bruce."

"Pleased to meet you, Clark," Bruce drawled, flashing his set of annoyingly perfect teeth.

"Bruce thought it'd be a shame if I had to eat alone," she added.

"I'm sure he did," Clark said dryly.

"A word of advice," Bruce said, talking to Clark but keeping his gaze trained on Blossom. "Never leave a beautiful woman waiting."

Blossom giggled, soaking it up. *Puh-lease*, thought Clark. How could an intelligent girl like Blossom not see through this pathetic act? It was incomprehensible.

Clark shifted his laptop case to his other hand. "I'm

sorry I'm late," he told Blossom. "But I really couldn't help it. Come on. Tell this joker to get lost."

"I can't," said Blossom. "We've already ordered. Maybe you and I could get together some other time."

"Fine," said Clark. "I'll wait until you're done lunch and walk you back to campus."

"Oh, no," Blossom said smugly. "That won't work. Bruce offered to drive me."

"Dinner, then?" It was difficult to force words through his gritted teeth.

"I'm working late."

"I'll pick you up at the college."

She shook her head. "No. Bruce and I—"

Bruce, Bruce, Bruce. "Forget it," Clark said tersely. "Just...forget it." He turned on his heel and strode off.

"Clark..." Blossom called after him.

He paused, hope slamming his heart against his ribs, not daring to turn.

"Let him go, babe," Bruce said. "He'll cool off."

"I guess you're right," he heard Blossom say a few seconds later.

Clark trudged on, toward the rear of the restaurant. He couldn't afford to leave the building, not with Bruce drooling over Blossom like a condemned man over his last slice of cheesecake.

He banged into the men's room, deep in thought. He needed help, and fast. But who...

That's it! He tore open the pocket on his laptop case and slid out his cell phone. No signal. Well, it freaking figured, didn't it? He just couldn't catch a break on this assignment.

He climbed up on a sink. Just as he got himself balanced, one hand holding the phone near the single window, high up on the wall, the door creaked open. An elderly man entered. He squinted up at Clark, then shuffled over to a urinal and unzipped his pants.

The phone beeped. *Yes!* Clark punched in a number and waited for an answer. He was almost ready to give up when a breathless voice answered.

"Hello?"

He didn't beat around the bush. "Diana. You've got to help me."

"Clark? Is that you?" A little laugh wafted over the wireless connection. "I thought you were on assignment."

"I am. And it was going fine. But now Bruce is in town and he's going to blow it for me. He'll have Blossom in bed before dinner."

The old codger at the urinal looked up from his business and shot Clark an interested glance.

Clark lowered his voice, trying to keep his footing on the edge of the sink. "You've got to help me, Diana."

He could almost see her inspecting her long, red fingernails. "I don't know, Clark..."

He was so not in the mood for this. "No games, Diana. You know you owe me."

The old man zipped up.

"Owe you? For what?"

"Programming your DVD player, for one thing.

Updating the virus protection on your PC. And what about last spring when I reset every clock in your house for Daylight Savings Time? What are you going to do in October when you have to set them all back again?"

A long silence, broken only by the flush of the urinal.

"Diana..."

She gave a little sigh. "Oh, all right. I guess I can help you out, if it doesn't take too long. I'm in the middle of something."

"What?"

"Shopping."

"Shopping? Seriously? When the world's about to end?"

"All the more reason. You can't expect me to face the apocalypse without a decent pair of heels."

"Well, where are you? Newark?"

"As if! I'm in downtown Megalopolis. "

Clark laughed out loud. Finally, a break. "Perfect. How far are you from MPI?"

"About ten minutes? Fifteen? Why? What do you want me to do?"

The old man shuffled up to the sink next to Clark's and cocked his eyebrows.

"Get lost," Clark told him.

"Well! If that's how you're going to talk to me—"

"No! Not you, Diana." He glared at the codger. "I was talking to someone else."

"Hmph," Diana said.

The old man dried his hands and creaked out the door. *Finally.*

"Clark? You still there? I haven't got all day, you know. I have a facial at four."

"You'll be done way before then," Clark assured her, and proceeded to outline his plan.

Saturday, 12:57 pm
Eleven hours, three minutes, and counting...

Clark had to admit, Diana really had a flair for the dramatic. And she showed up right on cue, just as the Sunrise Diner waitress brought Bruce the check. She'd outdone herself with the costume. Clark barely recognized her.

He watched as a shapeless woman, garbed in a colorless housecoat, waddled into the restaurant. He wasn't sure what Diana had stuffed under the housecoat to simulate an eight-and-a-half-month pregnancy, but from his position at the door to the men's room, her baby bump looked pretty damn convincing. Pink foam rollers stuck out all over her head and fuzzy pink slippers encased her feet.

Clark had lusted after Diana for years. In all that time, he'd never once seen her without makeup. Amazingly, without cosmetic assistance, Diana's looks hovered around average. Blossom's fresh, unadorned complexion was much more appealing. Clark mused over the discovery. Who would have guessed?

Diana, clearly enjoying herself, waltzed down the aisle. Then she stopped dead, one finger pointing at Bruce and Blossom, and let out an earsplitting shriek.

Every head in the snapped around.

"You!" she cried, marching up to Bruce and jabbing him on the shoulder with one finger. "You... you... worthless, low-life, two-timing *bastard!*"

Bruce probably had just that stunned stupid look on his face when he flunked his GED. "Diana?"

Clark chuckled. Old Bruce was pretty slow on the uptake. He didn't even have the presence of mind to pretend ignorance.

Blossom gasped. "Do you know this woman, Bruce?"

"Know me?" Diana yelled. She smoothed her hands over her impressive girth, arching her back and thrusting her belly in Blossom's face. "I'd say my husband knows me pretty damn well, wouldn't you?"

A purple-haired lady at the next table looked up from her lemon meringue pie. "I'd say so."

Bruce's eyes bugged out. "What the hell—"

"Oh. My. God." Blossom scooted down to the end of the booth. "You're married?"

"You bet he's married, Chicky." Diana held up her left hand. Clark noted her gold band with great admiration. He hadn't even thought of that detail.

"Well." Blossom scrambled out of the booth. "That's it. I'm outta here."

Bruce leaned over and grabbed her wrist. "She's lying. I'm not married, and—" He jabbed a finger at the stomach. "I didn't have anything to do with *that*." He glared at Diana. "It's a set up."

The lady with the purple hair laughed. "And if you believe that, girlfriend, I got a diamond ring I want to sell you."

"It's true." A hint of desperation crept into Bruce's voice. "She's not even pregnant. She's faking it."

"Right. Whatever." Blossom slapped Bruce's arm with her backpack. "Let me go."

"No," Bruce said, tugging Blossom back into the booth. "Not until you listen."

Shit. Clark grabbed his laptop and jogged up the aisle. He hadn't counted on Bruce getting physical.

"I said, let me go!"

"Blossom, I—".

Clark staggered to a stop at the table and whipped out his cell phone. "You better do what she says," he puffed. "Or I'm calling the cops."

"Clark—" Blossom said.

Bruce sent Clark a look that should have vaporized him. "I should have known you were behind this. Go to hell, Clark. She's mine."

Diana threw up her hands. "See what I have to put up with?" She pivoted slowly, working the audience. People were up and out of their booths, crowding down the aisle. "Do you see?"

"What an asshole." Ms. Purple Hair climbed onto her seat, craning her neck. "Honey," she said to Blossom. "Get out while the getting's good. Guys like him are no damn picnic. They screw you once and think they own you."

Bruce re-anchored his grip on Blossom's wrist. She struggled to twist free. "It's not like that," he said. "I can explain—"

"Let..." *Thwack!* "Me..." *Thwack!* "GO!" Blossom punctuated each syllable with a solid backpack blow to Bruce's shoulder.

Clark grabbed hold of Bruce's other arm, wedging his laptop case under the table top for leverage as he pulled with all his might. "You heard the lady," he panted. "Let go."

Bruce didn't budge as much as an inch. "Not until she listens to me." He winced as Blossom whacked him upside the head. "Jesus, woman! What have you got in that thing? Rocks?"

"You can forget me ever listening to you," Blossom fumed, angling for another blow. *"Let me go!"*

"No, I—"

Clark looped an arm around Bruce's neck and yanked as hard as he could. Damn. Nothing. The guy was a mountain.

"Allow me." Diana reached through the tangle of arms and put the supersqueeze on Bruce's wrist.

"Aaaaahh—" Bruce clawed at Diana's fingers with one hand. The other arm fended off Blossom's next attack.

"You're a sexist clod, Bruce. I don't know what I ever saw in you. We're through." Diana's elbow collided with his chin.

"Ooof." Bruce fell back onto the bench.

"You go, Mama!" Purple Hair yelled.

The crowd howled. "Come on," Clark said, tugging Blossom out of Bruce's limp grasp. "Let's get out of here."

"Noooo!" cried Bruce, lunging after them.

Diana crossed her wrists in front of her chest. *Uh oh,* Clark thought.

She spun around once, twice, three times. Her features disappeared in a blur as the revolutions picked up speed. Then she kicked out a leg, aimed straight for Bruce's junk. Bruce tried to vault the shapely limb, but agility wasn't exactly one of his supertalents. He stumbled and tripped, and face-planted in the aisle.

Diana scooped up Ms. Purple Hair's pie and dumped it on his head. Bruce, sputtering, heaved himself to his knees.

Diana jumped him.

"Ooof!"

The pair went down, limbs flailing. The crowd parted as they rolled down the aisle. Someone shouted advice. Somebody else called for the cops. The waitress shoved her way to the register and grabbed a phone. Ms. Purple Hair jumped up on a table and shouted a play-by-play.

Clark grabbed Blossom around the waist. He shoved her through the crowd, angling for the back door. His laptop banged against his leg as they scurried around a smelly dumpster, up an alley, and across Main Street. They veered right on Broad. Sirens sounded in the distance.

They didn't stop until they reached Blossom's apartment. Clark doubled over in front of the door, trying to catch his breath. A sharp pain sliced through his right side. He was out of shape, no doubt about it. Too many damn hours in front of the computer. He really should do something about that. Take up jogging, maybe.

Beside him, Blossom was shaking. *Ah, hell.* Bruce's caveman tactics must have traumatized her. A surge of raw anger made him see red. He'd get Bruce back for this. As a matter of fact, the very next time Mr. Wynn, *Superjerk,* tried to log onto his HUFF user account, he'd better be prepared for a fight.

His network connection was going down, down, down.

Blossom shuddered again. Her hands covered her face and her shoulders heaved. Clark shifted uneasily, passing his laptop from one hand to the other. *Hell.* He'd rather confront twenty Evil Maniacal Geniuses than face a single feminine tear. EMGs, he could handle. Hysterical women, not so much.

Still, he had to try. He reached out and placed an awkward hand on Blossom's shoulder. "It'll...uh...be all right?"

Her shoulders only shook harder. He took a deep breath and stepped a little closer, trying for a couple of comforting pats. "Blossom? Please don't..."

She looked up and laughed in his face.

Clark gaped. "You're not crying?"

"Crying?" she gasped. "God, no." She dissolved in a fit of giggles. "I've never...seen anything...so funny..." She doubled over again, fighting for breath. "...as when that guy hit the ground." She hiccupped.

Clark let out a relieved snort. "Me neither." He sobered a little. "I'm sorry I was late. The whole thing was my fault."

"No it wasn't," Blossom said quickly. "It was mine. I should have waited for you. I should've known things wouldn't work out with Bruce."

"Why not?"

She sighed. "He's too good to be true."

"What? Are you kidding me? He's not good at all! He's a jerk. A totally ripped, phenomenally handsome jerk, but still. No offence, Blossom, but you really need to rethink your priorities."

"You're right," she said. "I know you are. And I really try to like regular guys. I do. But the truth is, they just don't turn me on. I mean, take you for example."

Clark winced.

"You're great. You're smart, nice, and you have a good sense of humor. You really seem to like me—"

"I do," Clark put in.

"—but you're a geek and I just can't get excited about you. It would make life a whole heck of a lot easier if I could." Her voice rose, trembling dangerously. "I'm an idiot." She started blinking furiously.

Damn. Looked like those tears might materialize after all.

"Uh, Blossom—"

"I'm a loser, Clark."

"No, you're not. You're just—"

"Don't tell me what I am!"

"Uh, okay. Listen, Blossom—"

"Do you want to hear something really pathetic?" She couldn't seem to meet his gaze.

"No, I—"

"I've never even had an orgasm. At least, not a good

one."

"Yeah, I know. That's why—"

Blossom's head snapped up. "You *know?* How could you know? I just met you two days ago!"

"Uh, I mean, I guessed," Clark said, backpedaling as fast as he could. "I can tell you're a woman who..."

"Who what?"

"Um... You're somebody who wouldn't..."

Her volume rose dangerously. "Wouldn't *what?"*

"Sleep around," Clark finished feebly.

"Sleep around? I don't sleep around! Heck, I'm practically a virgin! How can you say that?"

"I didn't," Clark pointed out swiftly. "I was just trying to say—"

"I'm a mess." Blossom's eyes filled with tears.

"No," Clark said. He put down his laptop, inched closer, and draped one arm over her shoulders. "You're great. Fantastic. And very sexy."

"I'm frigid."

"You're not. I'm sure you'll have an orgasm when the right man comes along."

She sniffed. "You really think so?"

"Yes," Clark said. "All you have to do is close your eyes."

"Close my eyes?"

"Yeah. Close your eyes and listen to your heart."

Blossom sighed. "That's easier said than done. I'm a very visually oriented person, in case you hadn't noticed."

"I had," Clark said dryly. He maneuvered his free hand into his laptop zipper compartment. "But you know, if you're willing, I could help you overcome that."

Blossom's brows drew together. "How?"

He lifted a narrow swath of black satin. One of the purchases he'd made an hour ago. He dangled it in front of her.

"First," he said, "you tie this over your eyes."

Blossom stared at the thing. "You want me to put on a blindfold?"

"Yes," Clark said. "I do." She closed her eyes, as if imagining it. He felt a little shudder race through her.

He started getting hard.

She opened her eyes. "First I put on the blindfold.." She frowned a little. "And then what happens?"

"Then," Clark said, "you trust me."

Saturday, 1:39 pm

Ten hours, twenty-one minutes, and counting...

Clark's blindfold was black, soft, and utterly tantalizing. Blossom closed her eyes and tried to imagine how it would feel draped over her face. Blocking her vision. The bottom glided out of her belly and a soft tingling sprang to life between her thighs.

Clark's low, rich voice washed over her, sending little ripples of pleasure across her skin. "So what do you say?"

Silence stretched between them for one heartbeat, two, three. "I don't know," Blossom said finally.

He ran the blindfold down her bare arm. It was cool, soft, and oh-so-smooth. "Just try it. I'll stop whenever you say."

She believed him. He was too nice of a guy to lie to her.

She took the material in her hands. The center was wide, and double thickness. The ends narrowed into long ties. She held it up to her eyes, pressing the fabric flat, trying to see through it.

Nothing.

Only inky darkness.

She jumped when Clark's warm hand descended on her nape. "Put it on," he whispered. His breath was moist on her neck. The tingling between her thighs started up again, more urgent this time. "Go on."

With shaking hands, she smoothed the blindfold over her eyes and crossed the laces behind her head.

"Here," Clark said, easing the ties from her fingers. "Let me help you." With swift, sure strokes, he secured the blindfold.

When she reached up to touch it, he trapped her hands in his. "Just relax."

"All right. I'll try." It was a blatant lie. Having her sight taken away had started her heart jackhammering in her chest. No way could she relax.

She felt Clark shift behind her. He bent, as if retrieving something from the ground. His laptop, she thought, a little smile touching her lips. He was such a geek. But for the first time, the thought didn't disturb her.

He turned her, exerting a gentle pressure with his hand at the small of her back.

"Wait," she said. "First I want to know what else you've got in that bag."

He gave a low laugh. A rather sexy laugh, she thought. Funny how she hadn't noticed that about him before. She heard the scritch of a zipper. "You mean in here?"

"Yes."

"Just a few things I picked up on Spring Street."

"Spring Street?" she said. "But that's—"

"—a very, let's say, 'colorful' part of town." He laughed again. The sound made her want to lean back and melt into him. "I went shopping in a little store called *Lavish Love*."

She giggled. "That sounds like a porno."

"I think they shoot those in the back," Clark said. "In the front...well, you'll just have to wait and see. I mean feel," he corrected himself.

He kissed her neck, just below the ear. She hadn't expected it, and the suddenness doubled the sweetness of it. He nipped his way up to her ear and swirled his tongue around the shell.

"Oh, God," she whispered. "That feels incredible."

"It's only the start," Clark whispered. He pushed her gently forward. "*Now* will you start walking?"

She nodded. He guided her to her apartment, pausing to extract the keys from her backpack. Then the door clicked shut behind them. His laptop case thudded to the floor.

Clark's arm dipped behind her knees. She clutched his shoulders as her feet left the ground. He carried her through black space. It was a strange feeling. Like being adrift on an endless sea. She heard him kick a door open.

Her bedroom. She tried to remember if she'd left the bed unmade. No. When she landed on the bed, it was on top of the comforter. It puffed around her like a cloud, with a little whoosh as it settled.

Clark came down on top of her, the weight of his lower body pressing her into the mattress, his upper body supported on rigid arms. She ran her hands up his arms, along his shoulder, across his chest. Funny. In darkness he seemed bigger, more muscular than she had thought. And so much more solid.

He smelled nice. A hint of aftershave overlying a scent

of plain soap. She could hear his breathing—short, quick intakes of air. She spread her palm over his heart. It was beating almost as fast as hers.

He kissed her. His lips were firm, mobile. They tasted of mint. They coaxed hers apart, and she sighed, letting him in. Who'd have thought that a geek would know how to kiss so well? It seemed Clark was full of surprises.

His tongue plunged and receded. She clung to him, enjoying the sensation. It ended too soon, but she didn't have time to miss it. Her attention snapped to his fingers, which were undoing the buttons on her blouse.

Sudden fear stabbed her. She couldn't see him, but he didn't have the same handicap. Would he like what he saw when he undressed her? How would she know what he thought if she couldn't look into his eyes?

Her hand rose to stop him, but her blouse was already undone. His fingers stroked along the edges of her bra, then found the front closure.

"Clark, I—"

"Shh..." he said. "Don't worry. Everything's fine."

"I don't know. I'm not sure I want you looking at me."

His hands paused. "Why not?"

"Because... I'm not much to look at. No curves."

He chuckled. "Oh, I don't know about that." Her bra fell open and his palms cupped her breasts. "Looks to me like your curves are just fine. Perfect, in fact."

She felt his breath on her skin, then his mouth closed, hot and intense, on her nipple. She moaned, arching her back. Her fingers threaded into his thick hair, holding his head to her breast. He nipped and suckled, then licked a wet line to the other side and started all over again. Each tug of his lips and teeth shot a line of erotic fire straight to her groin. She moaned, and wriggled, trying to ease the pressure building there.

After a few minutes, he eased away. "I'm going to undress you the rest of the way now." His voice trembled. "Is that all right?"

Blossom's heart pounded into her throat. "Yes."

He eased her arms out of her blouse and bra, and then they were gone. He unsnapped her jeans and drew the zipper down, link by link. His hands were unsteady. Shaking. Cool air wafted over her as he moved to the end of the bed to slip off her shoes and socks. Then her jeans slid over her hips and down her legs.

Had her panties gone with them? No. He rose over her, easing his fingers around the elastic at her hips and thighs, brushing his thumbs over the swollen mound beneath. She groaned a little, pushing upward into his hand. He slipped his hands around her hips and cradled her buttocks in his hands. He drew her panties down her legs, inch by excruciating inch.

He moved away from the bed, leaving her naked, blind, and vulnerable.

"What about your clothes?" she asked. "I want them off, too."

"Soon," he told her. His voice didn't seem too steady, and that made her feel a little bit better. She heard his footsteps retreat from the room.

She shifted, trying to get comfortable on the bed, turning her head so as to better catch the sounds coming from the living room. She heard the scruff of Velcro separating. That laptop case again.

"Do you have a CD player?" he asked.

"Over near the TV."

A tiny cracking sound, then a click, a snap, another click, and a gentle whirring. The lush sounds of nature followed. Waves breaking on an invisible shoreline. The call of a gull, a rushing breeze. The surf pounded again, hard and sure. Blossom's body responded. Her arousal coiled a little tighter and she shifted, unsettled.

"Do you like it?" Clark whispered.

"Yes." She held out her arms in the direction of his voice. "Come here and I'll show you how much."

"In a minute," he replied. He moved around the bed again. She heard the laptop zipper. Another purchase from *Lavish Love?*

She heard a clink, then the strike of a match. The faint smell of sulfur drifted past, then a richer, spicier scent.

"Cinnamon," she whispered. "I love cinnamon. How did you know?"

"I didn't," said Clark. "I got it because it reminded me of your hair."

She smiled at that.

"What else do you have in that bag?"

More Velcro. Blossom ran her hands down her body, excitement rising.

The Velcro stopped. "Do that again," Clark said.

"What?"

"That thing with your hands."

"You mean this?" She let her palms drift down her torso, slower this time. She brushed the sides of her breasts, her stomach, her hips, then threaded her fingers through the curls at the apex of her thighs.

"Yeah," Clark breathed. "That."

"You like it?"

"Oh, yeah."

She did it again, starting from the top, this time lingering long enough to circle her nipples and stroke between her legs.

Clark groaned. She chuckled.

"You like tormenting me, don't you?" he said.

She smiled. "It's fun. I only wish I could see you suffering."

"It's not a pretty sight," he said with a soft laugh. He shifted off the bed, and again she heard the laptop zipper. "Here's something that'll distract you." He returned to the bed. The mattress dipped a little, rolling her toward him.

"Taste this." He brushed something cool and firm against her lips.

She opened her mouth. He dipped a rounded object inside. She skimmed it with the tip of her tongue. Ummm... Something sweet. Chocolate.

"Suck on it." His voice was husky. Low.

She obeyed, pursing her lips and drawing it in. An explosion of flavor burst into her mouth. A cool, ripe strawberry. Covered with a layer of thick, dark chocolate.

Heaven.

She ate it all, licking every bit from his fingers, and even sucking them a little afterwards. Clark groaned again, and leaned forward to kiss her.

"Please don't tell me that strawberry came from a porn shop," she said when she came up for air.

He snorted. "God, no. I got them at the gourmet grocer on Main Street." He reached across the bed, his arm brushing her legs as he retrieved something she could only guess at. "But I did get this at *Lavish Love*."

A soft tantalizing touch brushed her forehead, her cheeks, her lips. "What is it?"

"You tell me." He swept the unseen instrument down her arms, across her breasts, and over her stomach.

"A feather?"

"A long one," he said, stroking the crease at the top of one leg, then moving around to stroke the inside of her thighs. He lingered there, teasing. "Open your legs," he breathed.

She obeyed.

"Wider."

She did that too, quivering as the feather touched her again. Her inner muscles contracted, sending a faint glimpse of bliss shooting through her body. Clark ran the tip of the feather over her swollen folds, then played it over her tight nub. The sensation was too fleeting, too light. She groaned, as the coil in her belly tightened.

The feather retreated. Her hips moved, wanting it back. The ocean music from the CD player surged and receded.

Then the laptop's Velcro parted again, and her body went on high alert. What was coming next?

She heard Clark moving around—undressing, she thought. After a moment, he settled back onto the bed, down near the end. His warm hands lifted her feet and cradled them in his lap. His bare lap.

Blossom caught her breath. He was naked, in her bed. She wanted very much to see him. So what if he didn't have the body of a superhero? He had the heart of one. And he wanted her. She was beginning to discover what a turn on that was.

He began massaging her foot. He wore some kind of glove on one hand. It was slightly rough, but not unpleasantly so. Like a loofah sponge. "What are you wearing?"

He laughed. "I think it's called a bath glove. It's purple."

"Really?" She tried to imagine Clark, sitting on the edge of her bed, wearing a purple glove. And nothing else.

Her mind boggled.

He worked his way up her legs, his gloved hand leaving a tingling path in its wake, his bare hand soothing over the same path almost immediately. He avoided her breasts, and the slick, sensitive folds between her legs, moving close, teasing, then retreating without satisfying. The ocean music surged and ebbed in the background, a floating accompaniment to his attentions.

As he moved up her body, she reached for him, exploring him with her hands like a blind woman. He was surprisingly firm muscled. Not bulky like the superhero posters on her walls, but not soft, either, as she expected a geek to be. He must get away from that laptop occasionally, she thought.

Her hands slid across his flat belly and dipped between his legs. He sucked in a breath as she gripped his cock. Her fingers ran the long, firm length of it, all the way down, then all the way up again. The head was wide and warm. She cupped it in her palm, squeezing a little.

His breathing went ragged. He groaned a little as he leaned in and kissed her.

"You took off your glasses," she said. She tried to imagine it.

"Yeah," he said. "I can't see a thing."

She laughed at that. Her arms went around his neck, holding him tight. "Are we really going to do this?"

"If you'll let me."

"Do you have condoms in that black bag?"

"Only a couple dozen."

She smiled against his lips. "We can always go out for more later."

He levered himself away, until they were no longer touching. She thought she heard him strip off the glove, then tear a foil packet. She waited for him to return, but the seconds ticked by and he waited, not moving, not speaking.

"Clark?"

No answer. She lay still, waiting, listening. She couldn't hear anything beyond the ocean music—no movement, no breathing. Had he left her? Why?

The seconds ticked by. Blossom lay still at first, not wanting to break the magic of the game. But when endless moments passed and still he didn't return, she sat up, her hands reaching for the ties on the blindfold.

"Leave it on," Clark said.

Her hands stilled on the laces. "I thought you had gone."

"No," he said. "I'm here, watching you."

"Why?"

He gave a wry laugh. "I don't know. I guess I just like looking at you, knowing you can't see me. I'm not sure you would be so eager to make love with me if your eyes were open."

A glimmer of shame flashed through her. "My posters bother you, don't they? I'm sorry. I know it's silly of me, obsessing about superheroes. About men who don't exist."

"No," he said. His voice sounded strange. Uncertain. "It's not that. It's just..."

She wished she could see his face. "What?"

"I've dreamed of a woman like you," Clark said.

Blossom gave a shaky laugh. "You've dreamed of woman with freckles and frizzy red hair, who didn't want to date you because you drag a laptop around?"

He shifted on the mattress. "Well, not that, exactly. I've dreamed of one who trusted me enough to let herself go in my arms."

Blossom kept her voice steady. "And you think I could do that?"

"I know you can."

"I wish I could believe you," she replied. "But the truth is, I'm not sure it's possible for me. I've never had an orgasm. I can't even imagine it."

In lieu of an answer, she felt his lips on her stomach, her breast, her neck. His body moved, fitting itself to hers. She parted her legs, cradling his arousal.

And then he was inside, filling her, stroking, moving. "You know what I'm imagining right now?" he whispered in her ear.

"What?" she whispered back.

"The two of us on a beach, alone. Doing this." He thrust in.

"Someone would see us," she said. He eased out.

"No. We're alone. On a deserted island." He surged forward, harder than before.

Blossom sucked in a breath. "Are there palm trees?"

"As many as you want," he said, his hips flexing under her hands. "All around us. Swaying gently in the warm breeze. There are seagulls, too, calling in the distance."

"What does the ocean look like?"

He quickened his pace. "Pale green and sparkling. You can see clear through the water to the sand."

She felt herself slip toward something she desperately wanted to reach. "The sky. Is it blue?"

"It's brilliant." He was loving her hard now, with long, deep strokes, mingled with the scent of his sweat and the ragged sound of his breath in her ears. She opened her mouth on his shoulder and tasted the salty, slick flavor of him.

"The sand is warm," he murmured. "Warm and soft. You can feel it beneath you."

His hands ran along the backs of her thighs, lifting them as he angled her body for a deeper thrust. She knotted her hands in the comforter. So close. She could feel the moist breeze on her face, smell the salt in the air.

"Now," Clark breathed. "Do it for me." He gripped her hips and surged forward. "Let go."

Light shattered inside her. She felt her body fling outward, exploded into a million, glittering pieces, each one an eternal fragment of bliss. She clung to Clark's shoulders as his body pistoned against hers. She felt him go even harder inside her.

He cried her name as he came. His orgasm triggered aftershocks of her own release. They pulsed like the ocean, waves and waves of bliss, carrying her gently back to earth. When it was over, she melted into the warm sand, her mouth seeking Clark's lips. He kissed her deeply, his breath slowing until it matched the rhythm of the ocean in the background. A soft spray of water misted over her. A gull called.

Wait a minute...

Sand? Water? *Seagulls?*

She jackknifed to a sitting position. Her head smacked Clark's chin.

"Ouch!"

She tore off the blindfold.

And saw blue ocean and white sand. Sparkling sunlight. Palm trees. Seabirds. She wasn't in her bedroom.

Not by a long shot. A nauseating flip-flop of her stomach forced her eyes shut.

Oh. My. God.

"Claaaaark?" she wailed.

He grabbed both her hands and yanked her to her feet. But he wasn't panicked, like she was. He was elated.

"Hoooo-yaaah," he yelled, swinging her around. "We did it!"

Her bare feet fought for balance on the sand. She cracked her eyes open and focused on his face. He was very handsome, she thought, without his glasses. He should wear contacts, definitely.

Then she remembered she was in the midst a panic attack.

"We did it," he crowed again. "We really did it!"

"Did what?" She didn't think he was talking about sex.

He shoved the springy curl out of his eyes and grinned at her. "We teleported. From your bedroom to this tropical beach."

"Teleported?" It took a second to wrap her mind around that one. "But...that's impossible." She gulped. "Isn't it?"

He laughed and swung her around again. This time, Blossom had the presence of mind to be embarrassed. For the love of cheeses, they were both stark naked!

"Not hardly," Clark said cheerily. "Look around. We're here, aren't we? It's more than possible. We did it!"

He dropped her hands and punched a fist into the air.

She couldn't deny he had a point. This was not her

bedroom. They'd definitely gone...somewhere.

"But how?" she asked. "What did you do?"

"It wasn't me," Clark said. "You did it."

"Oh, no. No way." She shook her head wildly. "I had nothing to do with it."

"You did." He caught her hand again and tugged her down to sit with him on the sand. "Let me explain."

By the time he had, Blossom was stunned, bewildered, and seething with rage. And wishing desperately for some clothes. It was beyond awkward sitting here on the beach under a brilliant blue sky, naked, while Clark blithely explained how he'd been acting under orders from his commanding officer to talk her into bed.

Finally, she held up one hand, and he fell blessedly silent.

"Let me get this straight," she said slowly. "You're some kind of psychic superhero secret agent. I needed a wild orgasm to turn me into a superheroine. And you volunteered to give it to me? So I could help you save the world?"

Finally, he seemed to catch on the fact that she was somewhat less thrilled with this narrative. His eyes slid away.

"Um, yeah. Something like that. You know," he added brightly, "I think I know why you're so visually oriented. It's part of your supertalent. You need to picture where you're going in your mind before you teleport there. That's kind of cool, actually. Don't you think so?"

His earnest explanation was just so many words

jumbled together in her mind; she didn't even try to interpret it, much less answer. Tears stung her eyes. She blinked hard, willing them not to fall. She'd thought she'd attracted Clark on her own. She liked him, and she thought he cared for her, at least a little bit. Now she'd discovered she was nothing but an assignment to him.

She scrambled to her feet and started running across the sand. To where, she had no idea.

"Blossom, wait!" He jumped up and jogged after her.

She spun around and kicked a thick spray of sand into his eyes.

"Hey!" he cried, throwing up his arms to shield his face. "What's wrong?"

"What's wrong?" she yelled. "What's *wrong?* Are you freaking *nuts?* You talked me into bed under false pretenses! You *used* me! Well, you know what? You can just take your ridiculous story and shove it, Clark. Go save the world without me."

"What? You can't be serious. You have to help me. If you don't, everyone in the world—including us!—will be dead in—" He looked down at his nude body, arms spread. "Shit. No phone. No clock." He looked up. "Blossom—"

"No. Forget it. You'll just have to find some other superheroine to help you out. Preferably one who's not busy letting loser superheroes talk her into bed."

"If some other hero at HUFF could've stopped Lex Loser, the bomb would be neutralized by now." He spiked his fingers through his hair, leaving it sticking straight up. "No. There's no one else. The fate of humanity rests in our hands, Blossom. You refuse to help me...well, then I guess this is goodbye. Not just for you and me, but for everyone on the planet."

She stared. His eyes were deadly serious. "You mean, this psychic neutron bomb thing is real? You're not just making fun of me?"

"It's real." He placed his palm over his heart. "I swear. I know the idea of being a superheroine is a shock, and that you're untrained, but really, your part isn't very difficult. All you need to do is get us into Lex's lair. I'll handle the rest."

"Oh, that's all? Just teleport us into some supersecret underground bunker? How am I supposed to do that? I don't even know how I got us here!"

"You got us here because teleportation is your superpower. It's who you are."

She bit her lip. "But what if I can't get us back? We could be stuck here for weeks. Naked. With no food."

"There are coconuts, probably," Clark said. "But that's beside the point. You can get us back to civilization. I know you can."

Blossom drew a deep breath. "Okay. I'll give it a try. What do I do?"

Clark blinked. "I have no idea. Teleportation is not exactly my area of expertise."

"That's not helpful, Clark."

"Okay, well, let's break it down. What were you doing when you teleported us here?"

Blossom frowned, trying to remember. "Nothing

special."

"Thanks a lot," Clark said.

Blossom blushed. "I mean, besides *that*. I guess I was just picturing the beach you were talking about. And then, when I came, here we were."

"Okay," said Clark. "We can work with that. I'll describe HUFF headquarters, give you a mental image. You grab my hand, concentrate, and we'll go there. Simple."

"Uh, Clark?"

"Yes?"

"There's only one problem."

"What's that?"

"We can't go to your headquarters."

"Why not?"

"People are there."

He gave her a puzzled look. "So?"

"We're naked, remember?"

He looked down. "Oh. Yeah. I forgot."

Blossom rolled her eyes. *"Geeks."*

Saturday, 3:52 pm

Eight hours, eight minutes, and counting...

They landed in the bathtub, limbs tangled.

Clark lifted Blossom over the rim of the tub, trying not to get distracted by all the soft skin in his hands.

"That's strange," she said. "I was picturing the bedroom."

"That's not good," Clark told her. "We could have rematerialized in a wall or something. Or in mid-air. Your father was killed by an error like that."

Blossom shivered. "Oh, God. I had no idea. Mom never talked about him much. She told me he was a truck driver, and that he died in a big wreck."

"No, he died saving the world." He strode into the bedroom. "And I would really hate it if you and I died the same way. Ideally, you should practice. Do some safe, little jumps. Get the hang of it." He glanced at the clock on the nightstand. "But there's not much time for that." He retrieved his cell phone from his laptop case and checked the clock. "Only eight hours, seven minutes and four seconds to go. We've got to get to headquarters as soon as possible."

Clark grabbed his clothes, then scooped up Blossom's and tossed them to her. She caught them and dressed while he placed call to Captain Marvelous. He kept one interested eye on her while he updated The Captain as to Blossom's...uh...progress.

The Captain chuckled. "Good for you, son. I knew you had it in you."

Clark stood a little taller. "Thank you, Captain."

They had a couple hours before they had to check in at headquarters for their deployment briefing. Blossom used the time to practice teleporting from the bedroom to the kitchen, then into the hall, then out to the parking lot, then even over to an empty classroom at MPI. First alone, then with Clark in tow.

"I can never get to the exact spot I want," she grumbled.

Clark wasn't too thrilled about that, but he didn't want to alarm her by telling her so. She was already freaked out enough as it was.

"We can't delay much longer," he said. "The Captain wants us to report asap. Lex's bomb is set to blow in—" He checked his phone. "Six hours, forty-nine minutes, and thirty-three seconds."

Saturday, 5:17 pm

Six hours, forty-three minutes, and counting...

Blossom grasped Clark's hand, closed her eyes, and tried to envision the HUFF ready room, just as he had described it.

They landed in the dumpster behind the decoy sandwich shop.

"Fabulous," Blossom muttered, pulling unidentifiable muck out of her hair. "Just fabulous. At this rate, all I'm going to do is get us both killed."

Clark lowered his laptop to the asphalt, then jumped over the side of the dumpster and offered Blossom a hand. "No, you won't," he told her, but she could tell he was worried. "You'll do just fine. You're only a little off. The briefing room is directly below us."

"How far?"

Clark hesitated. "Thirty-six feet."

"Oh, God." Blossom's knees buckled.

Clark caught her before she could hit the ground. "Your long-distance accuracy is improving, you know." He steadied her on her feet, keeping one hand on her elbow and the other on the handle of his laptop case. "Come on. Try again. Thirty-six feet. Straight down." He added a few more descriptive details to her mental image of The Captain's ready room.

Blossom sighed. "Hold on." She shut her eyes and focused.

They landed right outside the door. "Not bad," Clark said bracingly, but Blossom wasn't so sure. There was more to this teleporting business than one would think. It required a heck of a lot of concentration.

Clark guided her across the threshold. The room was small, just big enough for a table and a few chairs. A tall, elderly man with a shock of white hair rose to greet them. Blossom couldn't help but notice that he was ridiculously fit for a man his age.

"Clark. You're right on time, son. Good work with the...ah...recovery of Ms. Breeze."

Good work. *Sheesh.* Blossom rolled her eyes. As if taking her to bed had been some kind of chore.

Her stomach twisted a little. *Maybe it had been.*

After all, Clark *was* a superhero. Oh, he may be a little on the underdeveloped side physically, but a lot of women wouldn't care about that. They'd be looking for the prestige of dating a superhero. Probably it wasn't difficult at all for Clark to find companionship. Probably, he slept with a different woman every night. Probably, they were all a lot hotter than she was.

Her stomach twisted some more.

"Ah, Blossom," Captain Marvelous was saying. "Good to meet you, my girl." He started to extend a hand, then drew back and wrinkled his nose.

"What is that smell? And is that a mustard stain on your shirt?"

"We had a small mishap, sir," Clark explained. "Nothing to get alarmed about."

The Captain frowned. "I see. Well, get cleaned up, and quickly. I'll need to assess Blossom's talent before you deploy. After all, the fate of life as we know it is at stake."

Saturday, 6:22 pm

Five hours, thirty-eight minutes, and counting...

"I don't know if I can do this," Blossom wailed.

She and Clark were standing in the middle of a very closed Megalopolis Museum of Natural History, in front of an enormous Tyrannosaurus Rex skeleton. "I was supposed to land us next to the Triceratops."

"That's the next exhibit over," Clark pointed out. "It could've been worse. You might have teleported us into the men's room."

She frowned at him. "Don't joke. I'm trying as hard as I can, and the best I've been able to do is three feet from the target. According to The Captain, Lex Loser's underground lair is a twisting maze of narrow passages. I'll never hit one. We'll materialize right in bedrock."

"His central lab is a large room. We'll go for that."

"And lose the element of surprise," Blossom grumbled. "He'll see us coming and blast us before you get a chance to defuse the bomb."

"Geez," said Clark. "Are you always this pessimistic?"

"I don't know," admitted Blossom. "I've never done anything this important before."

"Welcome to the wonderful world of superheroes," Clark said.

Saturday, 8:30 pm
Three hours, thirty minutes, and counting...

"Ready?" Captain Marvelous asked.

Clark glanced at Blossom. She didn't look the least bit ready, but unfortunately, their time had run out.

"Ready," Clark said.

"Go," The Captain said.

Saturday, 8:33 pm
Three hours, twenty-seven minutes, and counting...

Well, the good news was, Blossom didn't teleport them into bedrock. The bad news was, Clark had no idea where they were. They'd materialized in a narrow channel enclosed by rocky walls. He raised his flashlight and shone the beam first in one direction, then the other. Nothing.

A drop of water splashed onto his nose. He sneezed. The sound echoed like a thunderclap.

"I hope Lex didn't hear that," Blossom muttered.

Clark unzipped his laptop case and powered up the machine. If he could get a satellite signal, he could triangulate their location with his GPS receiver. Mentally, he depressed the required keys. "Come on..."

A "no service" message flashed onto the screen.

"Damn," he said. "I guess we're on our own."

"Not what I wanted to hear." Blossom had found out during her practice sessions that if she didn't know where she was, it was much harder to get where she wanted to go.

Clark zipped up his laptop, then swung his flashlight to the front and rear. "Which way do you think?"

Blossom closed her eyes and jabbed a finger at random. "That way."

"Right." Clark clipped the flashlight onto his belt and caught her hand. "Ready when you are."

Saturday, 11:46 PM
Fourteen minutes, and counting...

"Ah, Clark. I knew they would send you."

Lex's voice was casual, but the way his fingers stroked the buttons and levers on his control panel was anything but. Clark swallowed hard. He'd hoped to defuse the bomb before Lex noticed anything was amiss. Unfortunately, after three frustrating hours of bouncing through caves and tunnels like human ping pong balls, Blossom had finally landed them right at Lex's feet. Within seconds, they'd found their arms stretched overhead, restrained by robotically controlled shackles. And not just your regular, everyday, run of the mill titanium shackles, either. No. Lex had imprisoned Clark with...

"Magnets," Lex said, sounding inordinately pleased with himself. "Your one weakness, Clark. Your psychic computer-tampering powers are useless."

Clark supposed this was better than materializing in bedrock, but not by much.

"Only a few minutes until detonation," Lex said, squinting up at the foot-high digital clock on the wall above his head.

11:48:23 Eleven minutes, thirty-seven seconds to go. And there Clark was, strung up like a side of beef, powerless to stop humanity's destruction.

Lex chuckled as his fingers danced over the control panel. "We'll want to watch, of course." He pushed a button and a picture appeared on the flat screen overhead. Downtown Megalopolis, bustling with nighttime activity.

"You don't want to go through with this, Lex," Clark said.

Lex stroked a hand over his bald head. "Why not?" He seemed genuinely puzzled.

Clark eyed his laptop, lying useless on the floor at his feet. "Say your scheme is successful. Say you kill everyone in the world. What will you do for fun when there's no one left to terrorize?"

Lex's brows drew in. "A good point," he said, tapping his finger against his lips. "I didn't consider that." He laughed. "I guess I'll keep your girlfriend. That should be amusing."

Clark felt Blossom go stiff beside him. "Not an option," he told Lex. "You'd have to kill me first."

Lex smiled broadly. "That can be arranged." He reached under the counter and drew out a small caliber pistol. He leveled it at a point midway between Clark's eyes.

Beads of sweat broke out on Clark's forehead.

The trigger cocked.

"No," Blossom whispered.

"Oh, yes, yes, *yes!*" Lex said with an evil, maniacal laugh.

Clark's closed his eyes and braced for the end, a sharp sense of failure slicing through him. Some superhero he turned out to be. He should have let Bruce handle this one. Maybe then, humanity would've had a chance.

The gun's blast sounded in his ears. Clark's body went rigid, waiting for the pain.

It didn't come.

What the...?

He opened his eyes, then blinked to clear his vision. Lex Loser was sprawled on the ground, unconscious, his gun loose in his fingers. Blossom sat on his back, a startled look on her face.

"I did it," she said. "I really did it. I hit my target."

"Hit it hard, it looks like," said Clark.

"That part was pure luck. He smashed his head on the way down."

"Geez. You'd think an EMG like Lex would realize he can't restrain a teleporting superheroine."

"Geniuses tend to get cocky," Blossom said. "It's their fatal flaw."

Clark rattled his shackles. "The key," he said. "Find it. We've only got—" He checked Lex's countdown clock. *Shit.* "Nine minutes, seventeen seconds."

Blossom sifted frantically through Lex's pockets. "Got it." She lunged to Clark's side. Going up on her toes, she slid the key into the lock—first one wrist, then the other.

Clark stumbled forward. "Thanks."

"Only eight minutes left," Blossom said nervously. "Is it enough?"

"It'll have to be." Bracing his hands on Lex's control panel, Clark closed his eyes and sank his mind into the neutron bomb's computer trigger.

<password?>

"Crap," he said. "Lex's account isn't logged on. The system's asking for a password." He dove for his laptop.

"Can you hack it?" Blossom asked, watching him power up his code cracking program.

Using his mind as a network bridge, Clark linked his laptop to Lex's server, "Of course," he said. "Given enough time, it's a certainty. The real question is can I do it in—" He checked clock. "—six minutes and thirty seconds? I don't know. Lex's password is ten alphanumeric digits."

"That's 8.4 x 10^{17} possible combinations," Blossom exclaimed.

He raised his eyebrows.

She blushed. "What? So I'm good with mental calculations."

"I'll say."

She started pacing. "What are we going to do? It could take hours to find the right combination."

She was right, of course, but there wasn't much they could do about it. Clark watched the list of possibilities flash through the password field. So far, no hit.

Blossom stopped pacing. "There's only three minutes left. Maybe you should try a few manual combinations."

"Like what?"

She bit her lip. "I don't know. Lex is your nemesis. You've got to have some idea what he might pick."

"Birthday? Hometown? Mother's maiden name?" Clark tried them all. No luck.

"1-2-3-4-5-6-7-8-9-0?" Blossom suggested.

Nope.

Clark glanced at the clock. *Seventeen seconds. Come on.* What would Lex have picked?

An idea hit him. Mentally, he typed it in.

Hot damn! "We're in!"

"What was it?" Blossom asked.

"C-l-a-r-k-s-u-c-k-s"

His mind raced through Lex's system, picking up information. The bomb itself was hidden in one of the lair's upper passageways. Ironically, not far from Blossom and Clark's first teleport location. It was controlled by wireless pulse.

"Eight seconds," Blossom breathed.

Clark's brain rocketed through the directories on Lex's hard drive, searching for the bomb execution program.

"Six."

He found it.

<C:\documents\lexdocs\evilplan\bomb\bang.exe>

Originality had never been Lex's strong point, Clark mused. Luckily for humanity.

"Five seconds," Blossom squeaked. "Four, three…"

Clark dove into the system manager and executed an administrative delete command.

"Got it," he said, slumping into Lex's leather upholstered command chair.

Blossom squinted at the readout on the control panel screen. "Are you sure?"

Clark looked up. The countdown clock had frozen and

the plasma screen image of Megalopolis at midnight showed a couple strolling by, hand in hand, laughing.

"Yep," Clark told her.

"Then we really did it? We really saved the day?"

Clark pushed his glasses up the bridge of his nose. "You bet. With one-point-four seconds to spare."

"Wow," Blossom said. "Who would've thought?"

Friday, 10:35 pm

You'd think she'd be ecstatic.

Blossom leaned against the bar in the HUFF lounge, worrying the swizzle stick in her Long Island iced tea as she watched a free flow of testosterone. The room belched muscle. Corded pecs, bulging biceps, steel buns—you name it, it was here.

And a good portion of it was trying to impress her.

"So then I swung through the window," Peter Parkington was saying. "And knocked the kidnapper on his butt."

Pete was kind of cute, Blossom thought, but he seemed a bit immature.

"That's nothing," Dr. Banning said with a scowl. "Just last week I knocked a hole in a concrete wall with my bare fist and discovered a secret weapons cache."

A handsome man, Blossom reflected, but the green tinge to his skin was a bit disconcerting.

"Hey, babe. How's it going?"

She looked up, startled to find Bruce Wynn gazing down at her. Diana Price clung to his perfect triceps.

"I didn't know you two were still..." She drew a breath. "I mean after the Sunrise Diner thing..." She tried again. "I thought after Bruce ended up on the floor..."

Ah, hell. She took a gulp of her drink.

Diana laughed. "We're fine." She leaned in close and lowered her voice. "Bruce likes things rough once and a while. You should try it with Clark."

"Clark?" Blossom squeaked. She couldn't imagine it rough with Clark.

Bruce's moody gaze did a slow slog around the room. "Yeah. Where is Geek Man, anyway?"

"Not here," Blossom said in a small voice. And she didn't know where he was, either. It'd been six days since she'd last seen him, at The Captain's mission debriefing. She had a sneaky feeling he was avoiding her.

Diana confirmed it. "It's not like Clark to miss his own victory party. Or a free buffet," she added thoughtfully.

"He's a geek," Bruce said. "He probably got wrapped up in a Star Trek marathon or something."

They laughed and moved off.

Blossom set her drink on the bar, feeling suddenly sick. It was true, then. She'd been just an assignment to Clark, and now that the world was safe, he didn't want anything to do with her. Probably, he was out on the town, a tall, anorexic supermodel draped over each arm. Probably, he'd spend the night with them. Probably, he wouldn't give Blossom a thought while he was doing it. Probably...

Probably he couldn't care less that she was in love with him.

The bar phone rang. The bartender snagged it. "Yo. Yeah, sure thing, Clark. It'll be down in fifteen."

Blossom's eyes widened. "Excuse me," she said. "But was that Clark Kendall?"

"Yep," the bartender said. "He's in the computer lab. He wants me to send him a hero sandwich."

Sunday, 10:59 pm

Clark Internet surfed aimlessly, not even looking at what popped up. It hardly mattered. He couldn't think of anything but Blossom.

He'd known it couldn't last, of course. But somehow, rather than being a comfort, the knowledge only made his heart ache. Blossom was everything he ever wanted in a woman—she was cute, smart, and brave. She didn't give up when things got tough. And she was sexy as hell. He closed his eyes, reliving the moment she'd reached her first orgasm. In *his* arms. Her inner muscles had tightened so hard on him that he'd seen stars. That's when he'd realized he loved her. And when she'd saved him from taking Lex's bullet, the emotion intensified exponentially.

Then they'd returned to HUFF headquarters, and Blossom had immediately been swamped by every superhero on the payroll. They all wanted to meet her, hang out with her, hit on her. He'd stayed close, and heard five invitations to dinner in the space of seven minutes. Laughing, she'd accepted them all.

In that moment, Clark knew he wouldn't be able to compete. Blossom couldn't help her visual orientation—it was part of her superpower. And Clark just didn't look like a superhero. He never would. He wasn't even going to try.

He pushed his glasses up the bridge of his nose and

clicked over to digital TV streaming. An all-night Star Trek TNG marathon had started at nine. Maybe that would help keep his mind off his troubles.

A knock sounded at the door. His sandwich from the bar, most likely. "Come on in," he called, not taking his eyes from the screen. It was an episode with Counselor Troi's mother. He loved those. "Door's unlocked."

Footsteps, then a soft hand on his shoulder.

He swallowed hard and swiveled his chair around. "Blossom. What are you doing down here?"

"I brought you this." She placed a Styrofoam take-out container and a large soda on his desk.

"Um, thanks."

"So. This is where you've been hiding all week."

"I spend most of my time here," he told her. "I'm a geek, remember?"

She gave a soft laugh at that. "Yeah. I remember." Then, more softly, "How could I forget?"

Clark swiveled back to face the desk and popped the lid of his sandwich container. "You should go back to the party, Blossom. Everyone will miss you."

"It's your party, too. Come with me."

"No. I've got work to do."

Blossom sidled in closer, peering over his shoulder. "Work? That looks like *Star Trek*."

He hit the minimize button. "So what if it is?"

"So turn it off. Come to our party."

He couldn't stand being the object of her pity. "I know what you're doing," he said. "And I appreciate it, but you really don't have to. The assignment's over. Let's just try to forget it." He took a bite of his turkey hero, light mayo, no onions.

She inhaled sharply. "Oh. So that's what it is. That's all I am to you. A completed assignment. Somebody you fucked—"

Clark choked, spewing turkey and bread across his keyboard.

"—in the name of duty."

He grabbed his soda and took a gulp. "Is *that* what you think?"

"Well it's true, isn't it?"

He coughed. "God, no."

"Then why are you avoiding me?"

He looked up at her, slightly dizzy from lack of air. "I'm not avoiding you."

Well, okay, maybe he was, but he didn't like admitting it. "I'm giving you a chance to get what you want. A real superhero, like the guys hanging all over your apartment walls."

"But I don't want a man like that anymore."

"You don't?"

"No. I don't."

"Why not?"

"Why not? Well..." She gave a shy smile. "...because you're my hero now."

Clark gaped.

She looked away hastily, cheeks turning pink. "Look, I didn't mean to say that. Just forget I mentioned it." She inched toward the door. "I guess I'll go back to the party now. Enjoy your sandwich."

He leaped out of his seat and cut off her retreat. She collided with his chest. His hands closed on her shoulders.

"I can't forget it," he breathed. "I need to know. Is it true?"

She hesitated, her forehead pressed to his chest.

"Blossom..."

"Yes," she told his shirt irritably. "Okay? Are you satisfied? Yes. I love you. Now let me go."

She loved him?

"No," said Clark. "Not until you say that again."

"Let me go."

He grinned. "Not that part. The other thing. About how you love me."

"Clark..."

"Because I love you, too, you know."

She blinked up at him. "You do?"

"Yeah," he said softly, hugging her tight. She felt perfect. A reckless, joyful feeling crept over him. "Marry me, Blossom."

"What?!" She tried to twist out of his arms, but he didn't let her. "Are you nuts? You can't possibly want to get married. Marriage means car payments, kids, a mortgage, life insurance..."

"And sex," Clark said. "Don't forget the sex. Lots of it. Night and day. In every room in the house. Even the closets. In every position you can think of."

She blushed. "Oh. Well. When you put it like that, I

don't know what to say."

"Say yes."

Blossom looked into his eyes and laughed. "All right. Yes."

"Great," Clark said, taking off his glasses. He set them on the desk next to his laptop.

"Hey," she said. "What are you doing?"

"This," he said, and kissed her.

Thank You

Thank you for reading *Looking for a Hero*. I hope you enjoyed it! Would you like to know when my next book is available? There are a few ways you can keep in touch:

Sign up for my monthly newsletter at joynash.com

Visit me on social media:
facebook.com/joynash/
twitter: @sunflowerM0M
joynash.blogspot.com

Happy Reading!

Turn the page to read an excerpt from

Christmas Unplugged
Available Now!

joynash.com
excerpts, extras,
behind-the-book secrets

Christmas Unplugged
by Joy Nash

2 Brothers + 2 Sisters + 0 Electricity = 1 Unforgettable Holiday...because sometimes you have to turn out the lights to see what's right in front of you.

Excerpt

Emma peered through the windshield. "The turn-off to Dutch Gorge is coming up. Soon, I think."

"You're not sure?"

"Well, no..."

Casey sighed and kept driving. The narrow country road cut tight arcs through a forest of graceful white birch trees. The falling snow made things even more picturesque.

It was pretty, she supposed. Even if the rent-a-wreck subcompact car reeked of cigarette smoke. Even if Casey's phone had lost its GPS signal five miles of mountain road ago. Even if Casey had less than no experience driving on snow. Were you supposed to turn into a skid, or out of it? She could never remember.

Emma's blond hair fell forward as she studied the tiny map on the Dutch Gorge Lodge brochure. "Actually, I think we might have already passed the turn-off. It's hard to tell by this tiny map in the brochure."

The last thread of Casey's patience snapped. She hit the brakes...and felt her back tires slip to the left. She jerked the steering wheel in the same direction.

Thank God. She'd guessed right. Somehow, she managed slide to a stop without pitching headlights-first into the drainage chasm that ran alongside the road.

She snatched the resort brochure from Emma's fingers. "Here. Let me see that thing. All I need is for it to get dark, and I'll never find the damn place. Geez. You might have told me Dutch Gorge was in the middle of freaking nowhere! Any farther north, we'd be chasing down Canadian Mounties."

Emma sniffed. "But you have to admit, the snow is pretty."

"Yeah. Pretty damn dangerous."

Casey glared at the location diagram. Even as sketchy as it was, it was obvious they'd gone too far. Shoving the brochure back at Emma, she executed a slippery three-point turn. The snow—the beautiful, dangerous snow—was coming down in big heavy flakes. Casey switched on the windshield wipers and prayed she stayed on the pavement.

If they hadn't been so far from the state highway, she could have turned back. But the last town they'd passed had been miles and miles ago, and night wasn't far off. There was no way she'd make it back to civilization before dark. Surely they couldn't be more than a mile or two from Dutch Lodge. She squinted through the white.

"Finally."

The turn-off was barely paved, and all but

unnoticeable. Casey made the left, her muffler scraping ice as the rental car bounced in and out of a frozen rut.

"Lovely," she muttered.

From there, it was all downhill. Literally. Steeply. Apparently, the "Gorge" part of Dutch Gorge Lodge wasn't a fanciful marketing ploy.

She felt like she was descending into some kind of icy version of hell. At least the potholes provided some traction. And the series of hairpin switchbacks ensured she didn't fall asleep at the wheel.

"Oh. My. God," Emma breathed, one hand braced on the dashboard, the other clutching the side of Casey's headrest. "We're going to die."

"And to think," Casey said through gritted teeth, "we could've died in Jamaica. Lying on the beach. Drinking piña coladas. Why in God's name didn't you book a trip to the Caribbean?"

"Todd wanted to." Emma's voice trembled. "But I wanted a romantic white Christmas."

"You got the white part at least."

There were a couple of sniffs, and a discreet swipe of a glove to Emma's eyes. Casey, however, was in no mood to offer sympathy. Maybe later, when—*if*—they arrived alive.

Casey's knuckles had gone white. Her thumbs were numb. She might have turned around, if the damn road had been wide enough. Or backed up, if the damn road hadn't been so steep. As it was, they were in for one long, terrifying slide.

She rode the brake, inching forward as quickly as she dared through snow-dusted evergreens, the afternoon light fading far more quickly than she would have liked. She prayed the road leveled out before her nerves completely snapped.

"This had better be the right road. There had better be a lodge at the end of it. Because by the time we get to the bottom of this hellish ditch, it's going to be too dark to climb back out. They won't find our cold, dead corpses until spring."

Her sister sniffed. "Don't be ridiculous."

Blood pounded in Casey's ears. Her head, she was sure, was two seconds from exploding. "Ridiculous? Me? Look in the mirror, why don't you? Do you even have two brain cells to rub together? This has got to be your stupidest idea yet."

"It wasn't stupid!"

"It was! It's another one of your half-baked schemes. Bad enough you were going to drag that loser Todd all the way up here. He deserved it. But did you have to drag me into this fiasco?"

"Well." *Sniff.* "I'm sorry you feel so bad about— "*Sniff.* "—celebrating Christmas with your only sister. Your *heartbroken* only sister."

"Oh please, Todd isn't worth a single tear, let alone a broken heart. I'm just sorry he wasn't the one who paid for this trip in advance."

"Well, me too."

The road suddenly dipped, taking Casey's stomach with it. The car skidded for a good hundred feet before regaining traction on another hard bump. Casey wondered if her heartbeat would ever regain a normal rhythm.

"Damn it, Em! Couldn't you have at least rented an SUV instead of this death trap?"

"Excuse me for trying to save money! Anyway, there's no use complaining about it now. It's too late to go back up that mountain. We're committed."

"Oh, one of us should be committed," Casey said darkly. "I just don't know if it's you or me. How the hell did you find out about this place, anyway?"

"There was an ad in that free newspaper they give out all over the city."

"And just what, exactly, did it say?"

Emma half-turned toward the passenger window. "Something like...Get away from it all. Enjoy a romantic old fashioned Christmas."

"Lovely," Casey said again, grinding her teeth. A sharp pain shot through her jaw.

The paved road, such as it was, ended. Casey's wheels skidded on gravel. The snow-dusted evergreen boughs seemed to part before her, as if revealing some long-held secret.

Some secret. A small, snow-slicked parking area occupied by a battered pick-up truck and five SUVs.

"There's no sign." Casey scanned the parking area and the old stone farmhouse on the other side.

"No, but this is definitely the place," Emma replied on a long exhale. She waved the brochure photo. "See?"

The car slid down the last few feet of road. Too fast. Casey hit the brakes. Too hard. The car went into a wide, taillight-first spin.

"Oh, shit!"

The back tires hit a mound of snow. Casey's head thumped against the headrest. She jerked on the steering wheel, but the front wheels kept sliding.

They hit the snow bank, Casey's right front fender kissing the back bumper of a massive black SUV with Massachusetts plates.

"Thank God," Emma breathed.

Cautiously, Casey turned the wheel to the left and eased her foot onto the accelerator. Her tires spun. She gunned the motor harder. The tires spun some more.

"That's it," she said. "The end of traction as we know it. This rotten excuse for a vehicle isn't traveling another inch. At least not tonight." She sighed and opened her door.

To a blast of frigid winter wind.

Once again, lovely.

"Damn, it's cold." She hopped from one foot to the other as she fished her gloves out of her coat pockets.

On the other side of the car, Emma hiked her fur-lined hood up over her head. "But it's so beautiful."

It *was* pretty, Casey had to admit. Even—especially—in the falling snow. Like a Christmas card. The slate-roofed farmhouse stood framed by a steep wooded hill, smoke curling from one of its three chimneys. A covered porch sheltered a large bay window, softly glowing. A huge old tree, its leafless branches painted white with snow, spread its arms over the attic dormers. An old stone well adorned the front yard, and Casey could just make out the outline of a red barn behind the house.

"Look," Emma said suddenly, clutching Casey's arm.

"Emma. I've got to get the luggage—"

"Forget the luggage! Just *look*."

Casey looked. Two men had rounded a corner of the farmhouse, arms laden with firewood. Casey watched as they added the logs to a stack in a lean-to near the porch.

"Yeah?" she said. "So?"

"So? Ohmygod! Did you get a look at those guys?" Emma waved a hand. "Yoohoo! Hi!"

The men looked toward Emma, then back at each other. Casey thought they exchanged a few words before dumping the rest of their firewood and starting across the snow-covered yard.

"Oh. My. God," Emma breathed again. "They're even better looking up close. That tall one is gorgeous."

He was. Tall, muscular and hatless, with enticing, snow-dusted brown hair. Also, as far as she could tell, ridiculously handsome. Around thirty, Casey guessed. His long legs, encased in faded jeans, ended at battered tan work boots. His bulky red sweater, and the old Army surplus jacket he wore over it, were speckled with wood chips. Casey had no trouble at all believing he'd chopped every stick of firewood in the shed. The man looked like every woman's lumberjack fantasy.

His eyes flicked past Casey, and settled on Emma.

Typical. Guys always noticed Emma first. Casey was more than used to it. But for some reason—probably because of the harrowing drive down the mountain— tonight it bothered her more than usual.

But it wasn't the lumberjack who returned Emma's greeting. It was the other man—a bit shorter, a bit thinner, a bit less handsome, but still way above average in the good-looks department—who grinned and waved.

"Hello, ladies! Lost?"

"I don't think so," Emma said as the four of them met on the path leading to the front porch. The walk had been shoveled recently, but the new snow was quickly recoating the flagstones. "This is Dutch Gorge Lodge, isn't it?"

The men exchanged a look.

"Yeah," the shorter guy said. "It is."

"Then we're in the right place." Emma flashed him a smile, then batted her eyelashes at the lumberjack. "We have reservations for the Christmas weekend."

"Really?" Mr. Talkative asked. "Are you sure?"

"Well, of course we are! Do you think we would have driven all the way out here from Manhattan if we weren't? And I have to say," Emma continued, "the lodge is beautiful. It looks just like the picture in the brochure. So romantic! Just what we were hoping for."

Amusement flashed in the lumberjack's blue eyes.

"Well, then," the shorter man said, with an air of resignation. "Come on in, and Aunt Bea will sort everything out. I'm Jake, by the way. Jake Van der Staappen. And this is my brother, Matt."

"You two are brothers?" Emma exclaimed. "Why, we're sisters. I'm Emma. Emma Harbison. And this is Casey."

"Sisters, huh?" A sudden, wide grin blossomed on Jake's face. He elbowed his brother. "Sisters! Well, hallelujah. I am damn happy to hear that. Aren't you, Matt?"

It was the lumberjack's turn to look resigned. He

snorted and shook his head.

Casey was getting impatient with the brothers' obscure innuendo, whatever that was all about. "Um…you think we could take this conversation inside? Maybe before we freeze to death?"

"Sure thing," Jake said easily. He took Emma's arm. "Right this way, ladies."

Casey started up the flagstone path after them.

"Just watch your step," he said over his shoulder. "The walk is kinda—"

Casey's heel hit a patch of ice. "Aaaah—!"

She felt what happened next as if in slow motion. Her legs gave way; her upper body lurched backward. Her arms circled wildly, as if she could catch her balance on the frozen air. No go. She felt herself fall…

The arms that caught her were solid, strong, and warm. She blinked up, into the lumberjack's blue, blue eyes. For an instant, he held her frozen in a pose straight out of *Dancing With the Stars*.

"—kinda icy," Jake finished lamely.

And then the world turned right-side up again, and Casey's feet were once more planted firmly on the ground.

"Oh, God," Emma laughed. "I wish I'd caught that on video. Casey, you should have seen yourself. That was definitely one of your better moments."

Casey shot a dark look at Em's furry hood.

Jake quirked an eyebrow. "Your sister falls down a lot?"

"More often it's other stuff hitting the ground," Emma confided, one hand on Jake's arm. "She's terribly clumsy, poor dear. In high school, they used to call her Klutzy

Casey."

Heat rushed Casey's face. She glared at Emma, sure her eyes were spitting sparks. Emma smirked and tossed her head. It was obvious her sister's snarky little comment was payback for Casey's behind-the-wheel bitchiness. Which was probably well-deserved, Casey reflected.

Not that she was going to admit it. On the contrary. She was planning to kill Emma. First chance she got.

Jake's eyes cut from one sister to the other. "Ah, well," he said hastily. "Anyone could be a klutz in this weather. There's a wicked layer of ice under all this new snow." He caught Emma below the elbow. "Here, let me help you..."

Casey watched as the pair made their way to the farmhouse porch, Jake's arm sliding around Emma's waist. She fought an urge to roll her eyes. The Todd drama wasn't even forty-eight hours old, and Emma hadn't even seriously started fishing for a replacement. And here was one already gulping down the hook.

Matt cleared his throat.

She looked up, her face going even hotter than before. She could practically feel the snow sizzling as it hit her skin.

"Think you can manage the path to the house alone?" he asked. "Or should I carry you, too?"

She nearly choked. "Not necessary." Though she was fairly certain Mr. Lumberjack was strong enough to pick her up and throw her over his shoulder. That thought brought another rush of heat.

God. What a farce this Adirondack trip was turning out to be. She couldn't wait to hole up in her room and count the hours until Christmas was over and she could leave.

Good thing she'd brought her computer.

***

"Twenty bucks, big brother." Jake's grin stretched from ear to ear. "Sisters. Not lesbians."

Matt eyed the two women standing under the flickering gaslight in the foyer, chatting with Aunt Bea. With a sigh, he extracted his wallet from his back pocket and pulled out a crisp Andrew Jackson.

"It was a logical assumption," he said as the money disappeared into his brother's pocket. "Those two look nothing alike. And this is supposed to be a couples' weekend. Exclusively. I know for a fact Aunt Bea was not expecting three couples and a pair of sisters."

Jake shrugged. "Call it a gift from the heavens. A Christmas miracle. Jesus. What an angel."

He was talking about the blonde sister, of course. Jake had a thing for blondes. This one was incredibly beautiful. Big blue eyes, high cheekbones, bright smile, unsmudged makeup. She was incredibly busty, given her size two body. Or maybe she just had an incredible plastic surgeon. She did look...plastic.

By contrast, the other sister looked...real. A bit taller, a bit heavier, a good bit less round in the chest, and no makeup as far as he could tell. She appeared much less breakable. And much less pleased with life. She had smudges under her eyes and her lips were pressed into a frown. Her dark hair was a tangled mass of curls.

"Just let me remind you," he told Jake, "we're here to

work. Not to hit on the guests."

"I'll be discreet," Jake said. "Hell, I'll be anything if it gets me close to Emma. Man, oh man, does she fill out that sweater. And those legs—"

But Matt had stopped listening to his brother.

"...always wanted to act in the theater," Jake's blonde—Emma—was saying to Aunt Bea's interested nod. "On Broadway. So Casey and I, we moved to New York last spring. From Florida. That's where we grew up."

"You're a Broadway actress, dear? How lovely."

Aunt Bea glanced at Matt over her bifocals. Matt nearly groaned out loud. An aspiring actress? God Almighty, he should have known. She had the look.

"Well, not yet," Emma was saying, "but Broadway's been my dream forever! So far, though, I haven't had much luck getting into any auditions. I just don't know the right people."

"Oh, Christ." Jake made a low sound of disgust. "An actress. It just figures. If Emma finds out who you are, my chances with her are toast."

"Your chances and my sanity," Matt grumbled.

"Jesus, Matt, we gotta do something."

Matt cut him a glance. "Like what?"

"Like...I don't know, but something quick. Aunt Bea's thirty seconds from some very helpful acting advice." He frowned. "Think she'd go for bribery? We could promise to polish the good silver. Or chop another three cords of wood."

Not a bad idea, Matt thought as his aunt drew a breath to reply to Emma. Just in time, he caught Bea's gaze, and made a cutting motion with his hand.

No, he mouthed. Don't tell her...

Aunt Bea pursed her lips and turned her attention back to Emma. "Acting is such a challenging career, dear. It's hard to get started. It does help to know the right people." She gave Matt a speaking glance. "Or so I've been told by...people...who know the business."

Jake groaned. "That's it. She's gonna spill, and I'm gonna officially drop off the face of the planet as far as Emma's concerned. Though I suppose I might have a shot at the klutzy sister..."

"No." Matt was not in the mood to spend the next four days dodging the attentions of a wannabe actress. He reached the desk in two strides.

"Aunt Bea?" He slid a hand under her elbow. "Can I talk to you a moment?"

"Matthew! I was just about to tell Emma about your—"

"*Now,* Aunt Bea. Jake can take over the check-in."

A smiling Jake quickly stepped up to the antique roll-top desk where Aunt Bea kept her reservations ledger. "It would be my pleasure, ladies."

Bea frowned as Matt guided her to the alcove under the stair. He lowered his voice. "Aunt Bea. Don't tell that woman anything. Please."

"But Matthew, why not? Emma's an aspiring actress, new to the city, and you're always looking for new talent."

"True enough, but I just don't want to get into it this weekend. I came upstate to help you and Uncle Fred, not to add to my call list. Just keep quiet about the agency, okay?"

Bea was not pleased. "Emma's a guest, Matthew. And she seems like such a nice girl—"

"I'll have Jake get her number." Matt was getting truly desperate, to agree to that. He was one of the most sought after casting directors in the city—only one starry-eyed newbie actress in a hundred made his Broadway call list. Though he could probably swing Emma a TV commercial if she wasn't completely hopeless. She had the looks for it, anyway.

"I'll call her in for an interview and screen test after the holidays," he said. "But only if you promise not to say anything to her while she's here. And that goes for Uncle Fred, too."

The twin lines between his aunt's eyes deepened. "Well, all right, Matthew, if you insist. But I really don't underst—"

"Why are these sisters here, anyway? I thought only couples were booked for the Romance of Christmas weekend."

"Yes, well, that's true. But apparently Emma and her boyfriend stopped dating just a few days ago, poor dear. So she brought her sister with her instead."

Ah. So that explained why the wild-haired sister looked less than thrilled. She hadn't wanted to come. Dutch Gorge in December wasn't everyone's idea of a vacation, least of all, Matt supposed, someone from Florida.

He guided Bea back to the sisters. His brother's head was bent over the reservation ledger.

"You ladies are in the Daisy room," Jake said.

"That's our nicest room," Aunt Bea said. "Almost a suite. It's a bit of a climb, of course, up to the third floor. But it does have a private bath."

"It sounds perfect," Emma said.

"Jake," Matt interjected, "why don't you take Emma to her room? Her sister can show me what luggage to bring up."

"Right," Jake said, springing into action. "Emma, right this way. Here, let me take your coat. Casey, careful out there on the path." He winked. "Wouldn't want Matt here to throw his back out..."

Emma laughed. Casey shot a glare at her sister, before turning to follow Matt back out to the porch. Full night had fallen. The muted light shining through the bay window cast a warm glow into the dark. Even in the yellow gaslight, Casey looked pale. And tired.

"Long drive up from the city?"

She snorted. "Only about five hours too long. And then it started snowing, and we missed the turn into the gorge, and the road got slippery, and we got into a fight... God. I can't believe I let my sister talk me into coming out here."

"Ah well, at least you made it safely."

"Barely. Who built that road, anyway? We're lucky we didn't go over the side of the freaking mountain! I'm telling you, if we survive the drive home, I am going to kill that woman. Slowly."

Her voice was trembling. More from fear than from true anger, Matt thought. A delayed reaction to a drive that had truly frightened her.

"The road into the gorge can be dicey," he said.

"Especially in a snowfall. First northern winter, I take it?"

She shivered. "Yes."

"Driving on snow takes a bit of practice. But don't worry. You'll get used to it."

She made a sound of disdain. "I'd rather not, thank you."

Man, but she was prickly. With that frown and all that crazy hair, she looked like a disgruntled hedgehog. But even so...he scrutinized her more closely. Now that she wasn't standing next to her stunning sister, he realized she wasn't as plain as he'd first thought. She had the kind of look he'd have cast for a best-friend role. A pleasant face, with good bone structure. He thought her eyes were brown. Maybe. It was hard to tell in the dark. She was probably even pretty when she smiled.

She wasn't smiling at the moment. She looked ready to strangle someone. Her sister, most likely. He swallowed a laugh.

Production title: Sidekick. Woman perpetually trapped in her sister's misadventures finally snaps, revealing a dangerous violent streak...

He shook the thought out of his head. Christ. Hadn't he just told Aunt Bea he didn't want to think about work? Unfortunately, the drive upstate hadn't put the brakes on his obsessive habit of casting everyone around him into imaginary dramas.

The snow was coming down in a thick curtain now, the steady north wind whistling down the gorge. A rogue gust picked up a swirl of new-fallen snow off the front yard and threw it into their faces.

Casey gripped the lapels of her coat, savagely wrenching the fabric tight across her chest. Not that it was going to do her any good. The flimsy thing was designed for a city winter. Not a mountain one.

"God, it's cold." Her teeth were actually chattering.

"Actually, it's barely below twenty," Matt said, purely for the enjoyment of seeing her scowl deepen. "But it's supposed to drop to single digits tonight."

"Lovely," she muttered.

He took pity on her. "Listen, if you're that cold, just give me your key and tell me how many bags you've got. No need to come with me to your car."

"No." She hugged the coat tighter. "You won't be able to carry it all by yourself. Emma is not a light packer."

She stepped off the porch, tripped on the first step, and lunged down the rest. He barely managed to catch hold of her arm before she landed face-first in the snow.

"Wow. Your sister wasn't kidding, was she? About you making a habit of falling?"

She jerked her sleeve out of his grip. "I'm fine. It's just these boots. They're not the best on ice."

Matt extracted a small flashlight from his pocket. "Here. This might help."

"Thanks."

She plowed through the snow, following the thin beam of light, placing each step with care. "Damn it's dark out here," she said. "And quiet."

"That's the snow. It muffles everything."

They managed to reach her car without further mishap. "Nice park job," he commented.

"Bite your tongue."

He chuckled. "Another inch and Jake's bumper would have turned your fender into crumpled aluminum foil."

"I know." She climbed over the snow bank to open the trunk. The interior revealed a pair of pink suitcases and a worn navy blue duffle.

Matt handed Casey the flashlight and started collecting the bags, slinging the duffle over his shoulder and hefting the suitcases. Christ. The bigger pink one must be filled with bricks. He didn't have to ask who it belonged to.

"Your sister planning to stay the month?"

"Emma likes to be prepared." Casey reached into the trunk for one last bag.

"Might as well leave that one," he told her.

She glanced up at him. "What?"

"That's a computer, right?"

"Yes."

"Then why bring it in? You won't be able to use it."

She straightened, setting one hand on the open trunk door and trying to grip both her bag and his flashlight in the other. The beam bounced wildly.

"You mean because this God-forsaken crack in the Earth's crust is in a satellite blind spot? I already know that. My GPS lost its signal even before we started down the mountain. So I'm guessing there'll be no Internet, either. But that's okay. I can work offline."

He snorted. "Can you work without electricity?"

She froze in the act of slamming the trunk. Her eyes jerked to his, and even in the darkness, he could tell they were appalled.

"Without...*electricity?* You can't be serious."

"Perfectly serious, honey. Dutch Lodge is off the grid."

Her head swiveled toward the house. "But...there are lights—"

"Gas light," he said. "And oil lamps. Don't tell me you didn't notice? It's usually the first thing that guests comment on."

"No." Her voice was barely more than a whisper. "I didn't notice. But...what about TV? Hot water?" She sucked in a breath. *"Heat?"*

"Sorry, no TV. But there's plenty of hot water, courtesy of a mountain spring Uncle Fred piped in years ago. A large propane tank out back takes care of the gaslights and water heaters. And there's a fireplace or wood burning stove in every room. Don't worry, you'll get your hot baths, and you won't freeze."

"But—no electricity? How can anyone live without electricity?"

He laughed. "It's not so bad. I grew up here, you know, and managed to survive."

"But...but..."

The sounds of her sputtering shock made him wish for a stronger flashlight. "You really didn't know about the electricity? It's all in the brochure your sister was waving arou—" He cut off, and laughed outright.

"What's so funny?" she demanded.

"You didn't read that brochure, did you? And your sister didn't tell you."

Casey slammed the trunk. The crash echoed off the

sides of the gorge like a gunshot.

"No," she ground out between clenched teeth. "I didn't and she didn't. But she is certainly going to answer for it now."

Still clutching her laptop case, she flung herself in the direction of the house, her footsteps hard and fast. Well, as hard and fast as footsteps could get in six inches of new snow.

"You know," he said, juggling the baggage as he fell into step beside her. "Most guests at Dutch Lodge consider the lack of electricity a good thing. In fact, it's the reason most people come here. To get away from civilization."

"Yes, well, I like civilization just fine. I don't want to get away from it. No electricity," she added under her breath. "This is insane. That brat is going to die. Painfully."

That repressed violent streak again, Matt thought, impressed.

"She's just lucky I've got some battery life. If I make it to tomorrow morning, I might let her live."

"Why?" Matt asked. "What happens tomorrow morning?"

She spun toward him, stumbling, then catching her balance. The flashlight beam glanced off the white ground. "What happens tomorrow morning is that we're leaving. Whether Emma wants to or not."

Matt couldn't suppress another bark of laughter. "Leaving? Sorry to disappoint, but I really doubt that's gonna happen."

"Oh, it's going to happen, all right. The instant the sun comes up, I'm outta here."

The wind chose just that moment to kick up a wintery blast. "I'm curious," Matt shouted over the rising gale. "Did you happen to check the local weather report before plunging into the gorge?"

They'd reached the house. Casey stomped up the three steps to the porch before turning to glare down at him. "No."

He grinned.

Trepidation crept into her voice. "Why do you ask?"

"Because I was listening to the update on the shortwave just before you got here. This storm's turning nasty, and it's going to last all night. They're predicting two feet."

"Two feet?" Her mouth fell open. "Of *snow?*"

"Well, not of rose petals," he said. "So I'm pretty sure no one's going anywhere tomorrow. Least of all you."

About the Author

Joy Nash is a USA Today Bestselling Author and RITA Award Finalist applauded by Booklist for her "tart wit, superbly crafted characters, and sexy, magic-steeped plots."

When Joy was seven years old, she read a book about a girl who lived on the moon. She thought it was real until her big sister came along and messed up the story with the truth. Ever since, Joy's been of the opinion that fiction is way more interesting than reality. She credits her love of tortured heroes to the Brontë sisters, her fascination with magical adventure to J.R.R. Tolkien, and her weakness for snarky humor to Douglas Adams.

Connect with Joy
www.joynash.com
facebook.com/joynash/
twitter: @joynashauthor
joynash.blogspot.com

May the stories never end!